Madoda's
MAGIC

Madoda's MAGIC

To Catherine Middleton
Her Royal Highness the
Princess of Wales.

Wishing you the best
of health and happiness.

Frank Fontaine
18 Jan 2024

FRANK FONTAINE

First paperback edition 2023

978-1-80541-170-3 (paperback)
978-1-80541-172-7 (hardback)
978-1-80541-171-0 (ebook)

CHAPTER ONE

I often wondered whether I made the right choice to immigrate to the United States, leaving behind my beautiful home town of Rhyl in North Wales in the United Kingdom. I always considered Wales to be one of the most beautiful countries in the world, and I never dreamed of ever leaving it. Was it fate that influenced me to make this sudden move?

My name is Frank Mackintosh. I am 26 years old and I own this $30 million mansion in an exclusive area of Beverly Hills, California. Most residents are movie stars, wealthy businessmen, Arab princes and of course rich young widows enjoying their inherited wealth. One thing they all have in common - they are millionaires.

Since my best friend and I moved to this mansion we have become friendly with all our neighbours. There's a party going on every weekend. Of course, everybody wanted to meet the new single men with the funny Welsh and London accents. Once we settled down we decided to have a house warming party and get to know the neighbours better. The party turned out to be a great success, according to gossip afterwards. The guests loved the food, danced around the swimming pools, swam, and sang. It turned to be a wonderful party, enjoyed by everybody. We felt we hit it off well with everyone.

My dearest friend and business partner, Ben Johnson, also known as BJ, was relaxing a few feet away from me by the pool. BJ is black, born and raised in London. His dream was to become a heavyweight champion boxer. His father tried to talk him out of it but without success. BJ became one of the best heavyweight boxers in the world; he won the title four years in a row. Eventually he was hurt and the doctors told him it was time for him to retire. BJ made a lot of money from boxing and promotions. He was a smart man; made wise successful investments and soon became wealthy. He never married; he just enjoyed being single and free, which he bragged about and teased his married friends. Women were after him, but he preferred to be single. BJ and I became good friends from the day we met. I treasure his friendship.

As we relaxed by the pool drinking Chivas Regal on the rocks, I appeared cheerful, but did not feel good. I was not sick, but my mind kept wandering away, far away to my childhood years bringing happy and sad memories. I couldn't hide my mood for long. As I opened my eyes, I saw BJ staring at me curiously. I looked at him for a moment without saying a word, and then I turned my head away.

'Are you OK, Frank?' BJ asked.

'Yes BJ, I'm just fine. Don't worry.'

I didn't want to be disturbed; I just wanted to be alone. It was unusual for me to act that way, especially with BJ. BJ suspected that I needed to be left alone; he must have read my mind and he decided to give me some space.

That's one of the reasons why BJ and I have a solid friendship; we look after each other and help each other. We also learned to respect each other's privacy. And that worked very well.

Yes, there was something wrong with me. I stretched out on the chair, laid my head back, and closed my eyes. Before I knew it, my whole life started to flash in front of me.

CHAPTER TWO

I was born on 1 December 1981, in Rhyl, a seaside resort town in North Wales. My mother lived in Rhyl all her life, and she used to tell me that there was one paradise, and that paradise was North Wales. Rhyl was her favourite town. My mother always went to the same butcher, Mr Drake. He did not have children; his wife had a medical problem which stopped her from conceiving. My mother told me that whenever we went to his shop, he would rush from behind the counter to lift me out of the pram and play with me. My mother also went to the same bakery. Mr Hughes, the owner would make fresh rolls every day especially for her. His scones were the best in Rhyl. And then there was Ian, our milkman. He was very funny.

I remember when I was five years old he used to draw funny faces on the milk bottles that he delivered to us every morning. He knew I would be looking at them and they would make me laugh.

My mother, Catherine Thomas, was born in Rhyl. She came from a wealthy and respected Welsh family. Her father was Mayor of Rhyl for many years. He was kind and loved by the people of Rhyl. When he passed away, shops, city businesses, and schools were closed for the day for his funeral.

I loved my mother very much. I spent most of my childhood years with her because my father worked in South Africa. Every month he would fly from Johannesburg, and spend a week with us. He got two weeks' vacation over Christmas and New Year.

My mother used to take me to the beach during the summer. We spent plenty of time playing in the sand. Then we would take a walk on the promenade and have mother's favourite ice cream.

As I grew older, my mother and I would hike to the high hills and admire the beauty of Rhyl, the green grass and farms with cows and sheep grazing. I remember one sunny day, when I was 14 years old, my mother and I went on a trip to Anglesey. We drove as far west as we could go until we reached the lighthouse at South Stack. My mother had packed a picnic lunch consisting of finger sandwiches, salad, a variety of fruit and a big flask of hot tea. The weather was just beautiful with a light breeze, and you could smell the fresh air. How could anybody argue with mother about the beauty of North Wales. You just had to experience it.

On the way back home that day, mother drove to the University of Wales in Bangor. She stopped at the front gate, looked at me and said, 'Frank, this is where you will go when you are ready for university.' She looked serious, and was determined that I would get the best education and be like my father. My mother made sure that I learned all about Wales, and especially North Wales. She also taught me the Welsh language. She used to tell me in a firm and proud voice, 'A true Welshman must know the Welsh language and the history of Wales.' She was proud of her heritage.

My father, George Mackintosh, was born in Oban, a beautiful town in the Western Scottish Highlands. Oban has scenery beyond the imagination, especially when you go high above the town to Oban's Pulpit Hill, where you can see a fascinating view of the mountains, lakes and islands. My father came from a wealthy Scottish family. They always contributed generously to help the church, charities, care homes, and those in need. Just like my mother, he was proud of his heritage.

My father was a good golfer and he enjoyed playing in the famous St Andrews Golf Course. He played there whenever he had a chance. It was one summer, during a holiday in St Andrews, that he met my mother and they fell in love. My mother told me that it was love at first sight. A year later they were married. Two years later I was born. I was an only child.

My father worked as a mining engineer in Johannesburg, South Africa. He was called "'Mr Genius Engineer", and every large mining company wanted to hire him. He spent a month in Johannesburg and one week at home with us. He didn't mind the excessive travel, but my mother didn't like it. She was always worried about him working in the mines. She wished he would give it up and stay home.

We lived in Rhyl in a large mansion. My mother wanted it to be her primary home; she just loved it so much, and she loved Rhyl. That's where Father used to come and spend his time with us. We also had a house in Oban which we visited few times a year. I really liked both houses, and I was proud to be half Welsh and half Scottish.

The house in Rhyl was huge. It had ten bedrooms, two reception rooms, a large formal living room with a good size fireplace surrounded by an oak mantel, a spacious dining room with a table that could seat up to 20 guests. The kitchen was fitted with every luxury appliance, and there was a huge game room with a professional snooker table and a bar with dozen stools. My father taught me how to play snooker when I was young.

The house was surrounded by six acres of land. We had a full time gardener called

Joseph. He looked after the garden and especially mother's roses and other flowers. My mother very much enjoyed her home grown fruits and vegetables, like apples, rhubarbs, strawberries, tomatoes, potatoes, lettuce, cabbage, lettuce, and much more. The garden produced too much fruit so Mother would make rhubarb, strawberry and apple pies. She would make lots of them, and then give them to Mr Drake, Mr Hughes, Ian, the neighbours, the fire department and the police. And then there was Jane, our maid and cook. Jane was never called a maid; she was considered a member of the family. Mother knew her for many years and when her husband passed away my mother suggested she live in the annexe next to the house. Jane was there when I was born. She looked after me and she spoiled me.

My parents were modest people. Although they were rich, they never bragged about their wealth. They donated money anonymously to churches and charities, and privately helped those in need. I remember one day when my father was reading the daily newspaper, he saw an article about a woman in the town of Ipswich who had five children, aged between one and ten. Her husband had died from cancer. She was getting support from the government, but not enough to take care of five children. In addition, she was sick herself and required medical assistance. My father called the editor of the newspaper and told him he would send the paper £25,000, and asked them to please give it to the lady, but not to reveal the source. This is just one example of my father's generosity. He believed in helping those in need.

My parents were very much in love, and they adored and respected each other. Whenever they went out, they always held hands and stayed close to each other. My father loved Mother deeply, and showed a tremendous amount of respect and kindness towards her.

One day, when I was 15 years old, I wanted to know more about this unique relationship. 'Son, marriage is beautiful as long as you show love and respect to each other,' my mother said. 'You also have to be good friends, honest, and patient, and you must always discuss your problems with each other, never hiding anything. Also you have to trust each other. When you find the right girl with these qualities, you will both be happy for the rest of your lives. Love is kissing your wife every morning and before you go to bed, and always say - I love you.' That was my first lesson in love and marriage. I knew Mother and Father lived by those principles.

On Saturday nights, when Father was home, he would take Mother to their favourite local pub, where they met their friends, had a meal, and then spent hours singing Welsh songs and dancing. A 70-year-old Welshman provided the music with his antique accordion. He was also a comedian, always making jokes between songs.

To Mother, Father was her life; she loved him so much to the point where she wouldn't be able to live without him. Their friends noticed that, so did I. I saw her worried every day. 'It is dangerous working in the mines,' Mother used to tell me. She prayed daily that he would come home safely, and she couldn't bear being away from him. To make her happy, he telephoned her every night; they were like two teenagers in love.

Because I lived in such an environment, I grew up very attached to my parents. They were like my teachers. I learned the meaning of love, respect and modesty from them. My mother was a wonderful lady, the best mother in the world. She was my closest friend; she guided me when I needed advice, and comforted me when I was sad.

Father wanted me to follow in his footsteps and become a famous mining engineer. Whenever he was home, he would go into detail about his work in the mines. I was so proud of my father.

CHAPTER THREE

I attended private school in Rhyl and graduated with good marks. Now it was time to go to University. It was not difficult for me to decide which university to attend. I didn't want to leave Mother alone, and I remembered which university she wanted me to attend, the University of Wales in Bangor. It was about 40 miles west of Rhyl.

When I started at the University, my primary areas of studies were British History and Literature, and History of Ancient Egypt. It was hard work completing my Bachelor's Degree, but I completed it with honours. My mother was proud of my achievements. She suggested I continue at the University and get a Master's Degree.

My fascination with art and the culture of ancient Egypt started when I was 12 years old. Whenever I visited a bookstore, I always looked for books about ancient Egypt. I enjoyed reading about Egypt's impressive structures such as the pyramids and the Sphinx at Giza, and the temples of Abu Symbel which stood as symbols of ancient Egypt.

My father gave up trying to make me a mining engineer. He noticed how much I enjoyed Egyptian history, and being the type of father who wouldn't dictate my future, he told me to study what I liked best. Mother liked that very much because she always hoped I would not be a mining engineer.

I started work on my Master's Degree. My Egyptian professor was impressed with how well I did. He encouraged foreign students to study the history of ancient Egypt.

One of the requirements to graduate was to write a comprehensive and professional thesis. I decided that the best way to do this was to go to Cairo and do research to back up my thesis. My professor liked the idea. I spent three months in Cairo, and I completed my thesis. I completed all the requirement and the thesis which impressed the professor. I graduated with top honours in less than three years. My mother was so happy she planned a big party to honour my achievement, but my father could not come because he was busy working on a new mine that had just opened.

Unfortunately our joy did not last long. Two days after the party, my mother and I were finishing dinner when she received a telephone call from Mr Walker, the President of the company in Johannesburg, where my father worked. My mother immediately became nervous and started to shake. She was worried it might be bad news because Mr Walker never called home when Father was in Johannesburg. Her hunch was right. Mr Walker told Mother to come to Johannesburg as soon as possible because my father had been in an accident in a new mine where he was working. It was shocking news to Mother. She couldn't talk to Mr Walker, so I took the telephone and told Mr Walker that I would call him back. Mother sat down and cried saying, 'I knew this might happen one day. He should have stopped working in those mines years ago.' I rushed to Mother and hugged her. She could not control her emotions, and she kept crying and crying; her eyes became puffy and red. I wanted to cry, but I had to control myself and be strong for her sake.

I tried to console Mother but to no avail. She loved Father so much, and the thought of losing him was too much for her to accept. I knew she wouldn't relax until she saw him. That night we both couldn't sleep. We were worried about Father and were anxious to see him. I called the airline and made reservations to fly first thing in the morning. I also called Mr Walker and told him we should be there the next day. The next morning we flew to London Heathrow Airport, and then to Johannesburg.

Mr Walker was waiting for us as we exited Johannesburg airport, and drove us directly to the hospital. On the way, Mr Walker told us,

'George was working inside a new mine when an explosion occurred. Engineers and mine safety experts are still investigating the cause of the explosion. As far as we know 11 miners were seriously hurt and three were killed. We are told George was standing close to the explosion, and a rock fell on his chest and he suffered cuts on his head. George was immediately taken to the hospital, and underwent surgery.' Mr Walker was emotional, hesitating at times, trying to control himself. He then added, 'I can assure you that the best doctors in Johannesburg are looking after him.'

After listening to Mr Walker, it was apparent to me that my father's condition was much worse than we had thought.

As soon as the limousine stopped at the hospital, Mother and I got out quickly and followed Mr Walker. He escorted us straight to Father's room.

My father was in a private room. He was lying on his back, chest and head bandaged. As soon as we entered the room, the two doctors who were with him asked to speak with us before we saw Father. They told us, 'George is in severe pain due to head, chest, and other internal injuries. We did everything possible to help him, but we don't expect him to live. We suspect he is still alive because he wanted to see you.'

My mother was not listening while the doctors were talking; she was looking at Father, with tears pouring down her face. I knew what was in her mind - her husband, her life lover, her best friend, and my father was about to die. I gently put my arms around Mother's shoulders as we approached Father. She wiped her tears with a handkerchief trying to keep a brave face. She wanted him to live. She put her hands around Father's bandaged face and whispered, 'Darling,' a few times. My father opened his eyes and looked at us. He recognised us and smiled. My mother gently hugged him and kissed his bandaged face while saying, 'Darling, you will get well, just be strong. I love you very much.'

He slowly took Mother's hand to his lips and kissed it. That was the saddest moment in my life, seeing Mother crying from her heart, and Father in such a painful condition. My father turned his head towards me. He couldn't speak. He held my hand and joined it with his and Mother's, and then he stopped breathing. The doctors rushed to my father. Mother knew what had happened. She hugged Father for a long time and didn't want to let go. She then shouted, 'Please George, don't go, look at me, please stay with me.'

I slowly pulled Mother away from Father. The doctor examined Father, looked at us, and shook his head saying, 'I'm sorry.'

Those were words Mother didn't want to hear. She couldn't control herself; she hugged me and cried loudly. I was crying at the same time. Our feelings were mutual; we had both lost the most loving husband and father in the world.

That was the worst moment my mother and I shared. I was worried how Mother would cope without Father. She would be waiting for his telephone call every night, and she would be waiting for him to come home. How could she live another day knowing he wouldn't call or come home.

My mother didn't sleep that night. I was becoming concerned about her because she hadn't had any rest in the past two days. I wanted a doctor to examine her, but she refused. I ordered dinner for her in the room, but she didn't eat it.

Mother wanted to take Father home as soon as possible. She looked sad and tired the next day. I finally succeeded to get her to have her drink a cup of hot tea but she refused to eat.

I made arrangement to have Father's coffin and his personal belongings flown to London and then to Rhyl. Mother insisted that he be with us on the same flight.

That evening, just before we left the hotel for the airport, Mr Walker came to see us. He looked sad and was shedding tears as he hugged Mother. He then said, 'Catherine, I am going to miss George very much. As you know, over the years we became very close friends. We spent a lot of time together in Rhyl. He was like a brother to me.'

'I know that, and please come over with the family and visit us any time you want to.'

'Thank you. By the way, before you leave I want to advise you about George's financial situation here in Johannesburg. George was the most talented expert when it came to mining. The mining business has lost a genius, he is irreplaceable. He was also a very smart investor. George made quite a few investments during his 30 years working here in Johannesburg. We talked about our investments because we trusted each other. Since he joined this company he bought stock because he believed in it, and because we both invested in it, we both own a chunk of it. He owns 30%, and I own 20% of the company. Now, I can't give you exact figures, but if I tell you this, please don't be shocked. George has over £600 million in mining investments, and about £20 million in life insurance and other ventures. In addition, your house in Rhyl and the house in Oban are all paid for.

'So I will compile a list of everything George had and I will send it to you, and you can advise me how you want me to handle his assets. Also I will contact Mr Willis, George's solicitor in London. Maybe he knows of some other investments that George had that we didn't know about.'

'George did tell me that he had a lot of investments in Johannesburg,' Mother commented.

My mother noticed that Mr Walker was feeling sad and depressed. She approached him and said, 'I know you liked George very much and you will miss him. George liked you too. But George is in heaven now, looking down on us.'

She hugged Mr Walker and said, 'Thank you for all you have done. But promise me you will bring the family and visit us in Rhyl. Better than that, I suggest you retire soon and leave South Africa. You know George wanted you to move to North Wales. So don't wait until you are too old, enjoy your family while you can.'

'I was thinking about that myself. I don't need to work. I will take your advice Catherine. I promise to see you in Rhyl next year,' Mr Walker commented.

'I sincerely hope so,' Mother said.

CHAPTER FOUR

Back in Rhyl we held a memorial service in our local church. Mother didn't want a long service; she preferred one eulogy, which I did. Afterwards, we buried Father in the church cemetery. Mother was very religious; she wanted Father to be buried in the church cemetery because it is close to our house and she could visit him often. As we walked outside the cemetery, Mother turned to me and said, 'Frank, make sure that when I die, you bury me next to your father, as close to him as possible. So reserve the plot next to him now.' I knew Mother was still sad and upset and I replied, 'No, Mother, you will live a long time because I am going to take care of you.'

That evening my mother and I were sitting in the living room. We were numb with grief.

It had been a long day and Mother was tired. We loved Father so much that we felt lonely without him. Our housekeeper, Jane came into the room carrying a tray. 'Catherine, I made you hot tea and sandwiches. You must eat something, please.'

'Thank you Jane, but I am not hungry, I'm just tired,' Mother said.

'You should eat Mother, you can't go to bed on an empty stomach,' I insisted.

'Ok, I'll have a cup of tea and a biscuit, then I'll go to bed,' Mother said.

After Mother finished her tea, I held her hand and escorted her to her bedroom. Just before she entered the room, I gently turned Mother to face me and I said, 'Mother, I love you and I will always be with you and take care of you.'

I cried as I hugged her, and I whispered, 'Mother, I miss him so much.'

'I miss him too, very very much, Frank.

He will always be with us,' Mother said, and slowly turned around and entered her room.

I stood there for a minute, and then went back to the living room. As I sat down, I could not control myself and I started to cry. I was very sad and sick to my stomach to lose Father, and now I was very worried about Mother; she loved him so much.

I didn't get much sleep. I was thinking about Father throughout the night. And Mother, my sweet kind mother. I prayed to God and I asked him, 'Why God, why did you take him?'

The next morning I was having a cup of tea while waiting for Mother to come down for breakfast. It was after 10 o'clock, so I decided to check on her. I went upstairs to her bedroom and knocked on the door. There was no answer. I slowly opened the door and looked at her. She appeared to be fast asleep. I opened the curtains to allow light into the room, but when I approached her bed I sensed that something was wrong. I went closer to her, and took her hand, and I realised she was not breathing. I quickly telephoned for an ambulance and our doctor. I then opened the door and I shouted for Jane and Joseph. With their help, I tried mouth to mouth resuscitation, over and over, but couldn't revive her. Jane looked at me, and we knew that Mother was dead. The ambulance and our doctor rushed into the room and checked my mother, but they couldn't revive her either.

I could not control myself, and I started to cry, wiping my tears with Mother's dress. Jane came behind me and put her arms around my shoulders. She was also crying. We couldn't believe that Mother had died.

Our friends were devastated by the her sudden death, but they also knew how much she loved Father; she just couldn't live another day without him. They were like one soul.

We buried Mother next to Father just as she wished. All the guests were shedding tears; they loved Catherine.

That night I sat in the study with a drink in my hand. I was in a state of shock and disbelief.

Jane and Joseph walked into the study, also feeling sad. As they approached me, Jane said, 'Frank - your mother loved your father so much that she couldn't bear living without him. He was her life and she wanted to be with him. Nobody could have changed that.'

With my hands covering my face, I said, 'I am sick and confused Jane. I feel lonely. Losing both of them like that, oh God, why?'

Jane knelt in front of me, held my hands and said, 'I have been with your mother and father since they were married. I was there when you were born. So, you are not lonely. Joseph and I believe you are our family. Nothing will change that, and we will never leave you.'

'Frank,' Joseph said, 'we loved your mother and father. But now you have to be strong. You have a busy future ahead of you. You can't bring them back. They are in heaven now and they are watching you, and they want you to be happy.'

I was quiet for a minute, then I looked at Jane and Joseph and said, 'Thank you both for your support. You have been a great help to my parents. I am going to need you now more than ever.'

'What you need now, Frank, is plenty of rest. So don't stay up late. See you in the morning. Oh, by the way, I was cleaning your mother's room when I saw an envelope on her table addressed to you. Get some rest now. Good night.'

As I lay on the bed, I couldn't sleep. I kept thinking of my mother. Then I remembered the letter Jane mentioned. I got off the bed, and opened the letter. It was from my mother.

'My darling Frank. I couldn't leave you without saying goodbye. I knew in Johannesburg that something like this might happen, so I decided to write this, just in case it did. Remember, I loved your father beyond belief. You know how much we adored each other, and when I saw him there, dead, my body, my heart and my soul couldn't go on without him. I know that my heart will not accept another night without him in my arms and loving each other. So, if I don't see you in the morning, it's because I am having breakfast with him in heaven. And we will always think of you, you will always be with us. Promise me that you will follow the same tradition we lived by:

be kind, honest, loving, and considerate to everybody, and help people in need. We know you will find the right woman to marry, and have plenty of children, and tell them about us. We love you Frank very much, and will always be with you. Love. Your mother.'

I lay in bed, holding the letter on my chest, and crying. 'I promise you both, that I will live according to our tradition. You will always be with me, always.'

I woke up late the next morning. My eyes were puffy and red. I took a shower, dressed and went downstairs. Jane had a meal ready. She wanted to cheer me up, so she cooked my favourite, an English mixed grill consisting of a fried egg, pork sausage, bacon, beans, fried mushrooms, tomatoes, toast and jam. And of course a pot of tea. I kissed Jane on the cheek and thanked her.

'Did you sleep well, Frank?' Jane asked.

'Not well, Jane. I still can't believe what's happened.'

'Remember what I said last night, Frank,' Jane added, 'you can do nothing to bring them back. And now I want you to clean that plate, you need your energy.'

When I finished eating, I poured another cup of tea and went to Father's study. I was opening Father's desk drawers when Jane came in.

'Mr Willis is here to see you.'

'Tell him to come in, Jane.'

Mr Willis is my father's solicitor. He came in, shook my hand, and said, 'I want to express my condolences for the death of your parents. I'll miss them a lot.'

'Thank you Mr Willis. It's tough and very painful, but I guess I have to live with it. Now, how about tea?'

'No thanks Frank. I've just eaten.'

Mr Willis opened his briefcase and brought out some papers, and said,

'I thought this would be a good time to talk to you about your parents' wills, if it's OK with you.'

'This is as good a time as any. Have a seat.'

'Well, as you know it's quite simple. You inherit everything your father and mother owned. The mining company where your father worked sent us a letter. They want to know what you plan to do about his shares in the company. That's a lot of shares and a lot of money. Also, in the past 30 years your father bought thousands of shares in other mining companies in South Africa. These shares were very cheap when he bought them, and over the years, the companies did very well, and his shares kept multiplying. He never sold a share, and he never kept track how many shares he had. But I did.'

Mr Willis stopped to take a breather, then continued, 'Frank, your father was a smart investor. Did you know that this house is paid off, and the house in Oban is also paid off, and the house in Johannesburg too, and did you know that your father bought a large bungalow in Windsor not far from London, and that is also paid off. Plus he had a life insurance policy for him and your mother worth about £20 million. Oh, this is only your father's will. Your mother has her own money; all the money she inherited from her parents. That amounts to many millions. When I hear from the banks in Johannesburg, I will be able to tell you how much you have. If I have to estimate, I would suspect the total you will have would be approximately a billion pounds. Please don't have a heart attack on me.'

'That's a lot of money, Mr Willis.'

'Yes, it is. But you are young and smart like your father. Follow his footsteps, and you will be much richer.'

'Thank you for your advice Mr Willis. You have been my father's trusted and best friend since you attended school together. I trust you will look after me like you did Father.'

'I'll do my best, Frank,' Mr Willis said. 'You can depend on me. Now, would you like to make any changes, or do you want me to leave things the way they are?'

I paused for a minute and then told Mr Willis, 'Yes, I would like to make a couple of changes. First, please sell the house in Johannesburg, and send the proceeds to charities for needy children in Johannesburg.'

Mr Willis said, 'That's very kind of you Frank. And what about this house, the house in Oban, and the bungalow in Windsor?'

'Mother loved this house, so I'll keep it. Jane and Joseph can remain here and look after it; it's also their home. This will be my primary home where I will live. I'll keep the house in Oban, you know I am half Scottish, and the bungalow in Windsor. I will use them from time to time.'

'As you wish Frank. And what is the second thing you want me to do?' Mr Willis asked.

'Oh, yes, the second thing I would like you to do is to sell all Father's shares in the company he worked for, and all the shares he bought in other mining companies over the past 30 years. What I mean, Mr Willis, is that I don't want to have anything to do with Johannesburg. Sell everything he has in Johannesburg and put the money in my bank here in Wales. I lost my parents because of the mines, and I don't want to remember it. You see what I mean? And with your help, I can invest some of this money here in the UK.'

'I agree with you wholeheartedly, and

I will do just that. Give me two to three weeks, and I will give you a report.'

I walked to Mr Willis, shook his hand, and said, 'Thank you very much. I appreciate everything you have done. Keep in touch.'

Mr Willis put the papers back in his briefcase, and was about to walk out when I remembered something. I called to Mr Willis.

'Oh, Mr Willis.' He turned around.

'There are two more things I would like you to do please.' I walked to my father's desk, pulled a blank bank cheque, and I filled it in. Turning to Mr Willis, I handed him the cheque and said, 'This is for you, and I don't want to hear any comments about it. Nobody needs to know; it's between you and me.' I handed Mr Willis a cheque for £500,000 .

'Frank, this is just too much, it's amazing and very generous of you.'

'Mr Willis, I believe in honesty. I will always reward honest people working for me. No more comments, OK?' Then I continued, 'And the last thing I want you to do is this. Our church, where Father and Mother are buried. Would you please send them a cheque for £200,000 on behalf of the Mackintosh family. Well, I won't keep you any longer Mr Willis, call me any time you need me. And thank you for being so honest and friendly to all of us. Give my best wishes to your wife and children. God bless you.'

'Of course,' Mr Willis smiled and then left.

I spent the afternoon walking in the garden, looking at Mother's roses, and remembering how much she loved them. Every time I looked at a rose, I saw Mother's face, staring at me with a smile, as if telling me she was there with me, and she will always be with me.

I looked at my watch, and suddenly I realised that I was due to meet Jane and Joseph in the house. I took one more look at the roses, then I walked back into the house. Jane and Joseph were waiting for me in the study.

'Sorry for being late. Please, have a seat,' I said.

As they sat down, I continued, 'I have decided to keep this house. This is where I will live, this is my home. Mother loved it very much. I would like to ask you if the two of you would like to stay on, live here, and look after the house just like you did before. I will probably travel a lot, but this will always be my primary home. So, what do you think? If you need time to think about it, that's OK with me.'

Jane looked at me with surprise and said, 'We thought you were going to sell the house and dismiss us.' And with a big smile, she added, 'Of course we will stay on, won't we Joseph?'

'Yes, and I will always take care of the roses,' Joseph said.

'Well, that settles it. I am glad you agreed to stay on. And to show you my appreciation, you both deserve a bonus, so here is a cheque for you, Jane, and one for you too, Joseph.' I handed them a cheque each.

Jane looked at the cheque and with eyes wide open she said, 'But Frank, this is too much.'

'Please, don't say a word. You both deserve it,' I said, smiling. Then I added, 'And if you ever need anything, just let me know. Remember, I don't want you to owe anybody anything. We are a family.'

'Now Jane, I would like to have one of your delicious scones with fresh strawberry jam, clotted cream, and a pot of tea.'

Jane walked to me and hugged me, saying, 'You are just as kind and generous as your mum and dad.'

Jane was about to cry when Joseph looked at her smiling, and said, 'Let's get the tea, enough of that.'

As they walked out, I thought how fortunate I was to have such a loyal staff. I told myself that I would always love Jane and Joseph, and I would take care of them.

Fifteen minutes later Jane brought a tray with scones and tea. It was simply delicious.

I spent the afternoon in Father's study browsing through papers and notes. After a while I fixed myself a Chivas Regal on the rocks and sat on the Chesterfield leather couch. I didn't know what to do; I felt lonely. I didn't see Jane watching me, but she was there, bless her heart. She wanted to make sure I was managing.

Jane walked towards me and said, 'Frank, I have been very busy today, and I don't feel too good. I won't be able to cook dinner tonight.'

'That's alright, Jane. You go and have the afternoon off, and I'll fix myself something later on.'

'You don't have to do that, Frank. Why don't you go to your parents' favourite pub down the road. Tom will take good care of you,' Jane suggested.

'That's an excellent idea, Jane. I'll do just that. Thank you.'

Jane smiled and then walked out. I couldn't help but think that Jane did that on purpose. No matter what happened in the past, Jane always cooked dinner. She knew I needed to get out of the house, so she made the excuse. I was sure she would fix me a salad and put it in the refrigerator just in case I become hungry later on. Jane was so thoughtful and had such a kind heart. I was feeling tired, so I went to my bedroom and took a short nap.

It was dark when I woke up. I looked at the clock; it read 7. I didn't want to eat late, so I got dressed quickly and put on a heavy coat. I remembered the weatherman announcing that it would be windy and cool, and we might have some rain.

The pub was few hundred yards from the house overlooking the beach, so I decided to walk. As I entered the pub, Tom, the owner, rushed out from behind the bar, shook my hand and told me how sorry he felt about my parents. I then walked with Tom to the bar, while giving my regards to the patrons. Tom poured me a pint of bitter, the only beer I enjoyed.

I was always busy with my studies, so I only visited the pub few times a year. I looked around the pub admiring the way it was decorated. There were large and small paintings of old ships and warplanes framed with antique wood, hanging on the walls.

Various old knick-knacks were on top of the two fireplace mantels. The walls were covered with old English wallpaper, and there were dark wooden panels fixed to the ceilings. Different size Welsh wood spoons were also hung around. The bar serving area was in the centre of the pub, in a circular shape. Beer glasses from all over the world were also hung around the bar. And you could hear the sound of Welsh songs in the background. No wonder my parents liked this pub; it had a genuine Welsh atmosphere. I had just finished my pint of bitter when Tom asked me if I wanted to eat the finest fish and chips in Wales.

'How can I refuse that. Father always bragged about it, so I must try it.'

'Here's another pint of bitter, enjoy it while I bring your food,' Tom said.

Tom was excited, and he rushed to the kitchen, and before long he came out holding a platter with a large piece of cod, mushy peas, and chips.

Father was right. He used to tell everybody, 'You can eat fish all over the world, but you never tasted fish like you get in North Wales.' It was simply delicious and I ate every bit of it. I had another pint of bitter while joining the patrons singing Welsh songs. I was feeling tipsy, so I thanked Tom, bid him goodnight and left the pub.

Outside, the clouds were building and it looked like it was going to rain. I put my coat on and started walking towards home. I walked few steps when two men approached me. I thought they wanted to ask me for cigarettes or a match, but instead one of them twisted my right arm behind my back while the other one pulled a knife and pointed it to my throat and demanded my wallet. Without waiting for me to talk, he hit me in my stomach. I went down on my knees with my hands on my stomach; I was in terrible pain.

It was dark and I couldn't see well. But when I lifted my head up, I saw this figure of a man holding the two men off the ground, one in each hand. I did not recognise the big man, but I heard him telling the two men, 'Now, why do you have to beat on this fellow? Would you like me to do the same to you? How about I break all your fingers and you won't be able to work or steal anymore?'

The two men looked at him, frightened with their eyes wide, and pleaded with him, 'No, please BJ, we didn't mean to hurt him.' They appeared to know this man called BJ. BJ then pulled them close to his face and told them in a mean loud voice, 'I will only let you down and not break your bones on one condition. Kneel in front this man and apologise to him.'

They both shook their heads and agreed. BJ put them down. They knelt in front of me and they apologised. I accepted their apology, and told them, 'You are not from Rhyl, because Rhyl doesn't have people like you. This is a peaceful town, so I suggest you leave town right now, and never come back. I know what you look like, so if I ever see you here again, you will end up in jail.'

They looked at us, and then ran away quickly.

BJ helped me stand up and clear the dirt off my coat. As I looked up I recognised this big man called BJ; he was the famous English heavyweight boxing champion.

'Thanks BJ. Thanks for your help. I couldn't fight them back with the knife pointed at my throat. You came at the right time.'

'Are you alright?' BJ asked, touching my shoulder.

'Other than some pain in my stomach, I'm OK,' I replied.

I was glad to have such a giant helping me. To show my appreciation, I invited BJ to my house for a drink. He accepted my invitation and we went to my house in his car.

BJ whistled in admiration as we entered my house, and said, 'What a beautiful house this is.'

I was honoured to have BJ in my house. He seemed to be a nice gentleman. I asked him what he would like to drink, and he replied, 'Chivas Regal on the rocks.'

'You have an excellent taste, BJ. That's my favourite drink too. You know BJ, I didn't recognise you at first; it was dark. So, what are you doing in north Wales, so far from London?'

'I needed a break, to relax and get away from the London crowd, so my friend invited me to spend few days with him. I'll be returning to London the day after tomorrow.'

'By the way BJ, and sorry to ask, are you married?'

'No, never. I have seen many of my friends jump and marry the first girl they think they are in love with. Few years after that, they end up in divorce. No, Frank. I would prefer to take my time, and find the right girl first, then decide. That's safer. Marriage is not a game. That's how I feel about it.'

After a pause, BJ had a sip of Chivas Regal, and asked Frank, 'What are you doing in a big house like this. Do you live alone?'

I took a sip of scotch, put the glass on the table and said, 'Up to few days ago, I had a mother and a father, the best parents you have ever seen. My father was a famous mining engineer working in Johannesburg. There was an accident in a new mine he was working on, and he died. My father and mother loved each other so much, that my mother could not live without him, so she died two days later. Now, I am rich millionaire, but a very unhappy man and lonely. And I loved them deeply. I don't know how to live without them.'

'Frank, I am sorry to hear about your parents. I am sure many people have told you that we don't control our lives, someone up there does that. It's fate. So, please don't feel sad and lonely. Let's live our lives in the best possible way. You have to go back and learn to live the way your parents taught you, and the way they want you to live now. They're probably watching you suffer and feeling sad. They want you to enjoy life, they want you to come and talk to them every week, but they don't want you to suffer, they want you to be happy.'

BJ stayed quite for few minutes, he knew I was thinking of what he said, and wanted to give me time to think about it. BJ kept quiet for a minute, then he said, 'Frank, cheer up and tell me about your future plans, considering you are rich and single just like me.'

'I haven't made up my mind yet,' I told BJ. 'It has been a short time since I lost my parents. You raised good points which I will definitely consider. I don't want to waste my money just because I am rich. Maybe I could get into business, or maybe become a private investigator, or anything that keeps me busy.'

BJ laughed and said, 'You know, Frank, I also had an ambition to be a private investigator. When I was young, I used to go to the gym and lifts weights. One day, a boxing promotor saw me and told me that I should think of becoming a professional boxer. I believed him and I started to train with him. I told myself to hold off on becoming a private investigator. So I worked hard and became world boxing champion and I made millions. I became a millionaire. I invested my money wisely, and made a lot of money. I have now retired from boxing. So being a private investigator is not a bad idea; it would be exciting.'

It started to rain, so BJ decided it was time to go. We agreed to meet the next day at the pub for lunch. I liked BJ and I hoped we would become friends. He appeared to be a friendly person, and someone I could trust.

Was it fate that brought us together?

CHAPTER FIVE

The next day was sunny and bright. It was about 11 o'clock when I went downstairs.

'Are you ready for breakfast, or should I say brunch?'

'I'd better not eat, Jane. I have a luncheon engagement in the pub at noon. But I'll have a cup of tea instead.'

'Did you have a good time last night?' Jane asked.

'I sure did. I had some tasty cod and chips, and drank three pints of bitter. I felt tipsy because that's more than I normally drink. I also met a man you don't expect to see around this part of the country.'

'And who would that be?' she asked.

'Have you heard of a famous champion boxer, goes by the name of BJ?'

'Yes, a tall handsome man. How lucky of you to meet him.'

'He is a wonderful man. He is the one I am going to meet at the pub at noon.'

'You should have brought him here, he would have enjoyed my food. Maybe next time. Now you better hurry up Frank. It's almost noon,' Jane reminded me.

I hurried out of the house. BJ was waiting for me. We had cod and chips and mushy peas, and had two pints of bitter.

'You must have enjoyed your lunch, BJ. You ate every bit on your plate.'

'Yes, I did,' BJ said while rubbing his stomach with his hands, 'that fish was excellent.'

BJ pulled his chair towards the table, brought his head closer to me, and said, 'Private investigator - huh. You know, Frank, I kept thinking about that all night.' He paused for few seconds, looked right and left, then continued, 'I believe in fate, Frank, and I believe that fate brought us together. Here is what I want to say, since we both like to help people in need, and since we are both single, handsome, and filthy rich, why don't we start our own private investigation business. We don't need the money, but it would be fun. What do you think, Frank?'

I thought about it for a minute, and then said, 'Well I didn't expect to get into the business so quickly, but I also believe in fate. I also think it would be fun. Let's do it.'

BJ asked, 'Where do you think we should start our first venture, here in England or somewhere else?'

'I don't think it would work in England. The British people don't usually hire private investigators. But the Americans like to hire private investigators; it's a way of life. So, I suggest we go to America.'

We both paused to think. Suddenly BJ said, 'I agree with you. And I recommend Beverly Hills, California. I've heard about that place. It's is crowded with rich people, and any time they suspect something, they hire private investigators. Ah, don't forget the warm weather and lots of beautiful women too. Do you agree?'

I smiled and said, 'I agree, BJ. Beverly Hills would be the perfect place to start the business.'

So that's what we did.

We needed time to sort out our personal business in England before jetting to the United States. We figured it would take us about four weeks. It wasn't difficult for us to get visas, since we were both rich and able to sponsor ourselves. Besides, BJ was so famous that there was no delay in getting our visas at the American Embassy.

I met with Jane and Joseph in the study to tell them what I was planning to do. They were happy for us.

Jane asked, 'Are you going to sell this house?'

'Oh, no Jane, never. I will never sell this house, its Mother's. Like I told you both before, I would like for you and Joseph to continue living here, and take care of the house. I will keep you aware of my whereabouts all the time, and if you need me to come home for any reason, I will come. I will also pay for all expenses here. You don't have to spend a penny. What do you think?'

Joseph looked sad, but he put on a brave face and said, 'That would be great, Frank. Don't worry, we'll be here and look after everything. We are happy for you.'

'Just give us a call once in a while Frank. Don't forget,' Jane commented.

'Of course I will. You are my family, and I love you.'

They smiled as they left the study.

I then called Mr Willis, and told him about going to Beverly Hills. He told me that he had done everything I told him do, and he had the report that listed all my assets, and money. Just as he estimated, it was close to a billion pounds.

The day before I left Rhyl, I went to visit Mother and Father at the cemetery. I said few prayers and laid roses on their graves. I will always think of them.

I said goodbye to Jane and Joseph. I asked them to take flowers to the cemetery every week. They agreed.

BJ and I met at Heathrow Airport. We had a drink at the bar before we boarded the British Airways direct flight 747, first class, to Los Angeles. The flight was great; we couldn't have asked for a better service. We had reserved a limousine to pick us up at Los Angeles airport and take us to the Beverly Hills Hotel. After a few days of rest, we decided to look for a house to buy.

I thought the hotel manager might be the best person to ask about a good real estate agent. He suggested we contact Mrs Desmond from Hilton Century Real Estate. She was supposed to be the best in Beverly Hills. If you wanted a certain type of house, she would be the one to get it for you.

I called Mrs Desmond and in less than an hour she knocked on my hotel door. She was about 45 years old, wore thick glasses, had long black hair, and wore an expensive suit. She drove us in her new Mercedes, and showed us many houses. Unfortunately, we didn't like any of them.

BJ and I were getting tired, so we asked Mrs Desmond to take us back to the hotel and we would start again the next day.

'If you don't mind,' Mrs Desmond said, 'I have one more place to show you. I think you will like it, but it is very expensive. It is located in an exclusive area of Beverly Hills.'

We didn't say anything. A few minutes later she stopped, and pointed at a huge house high on a hill.

She said, 'This is the best mansion on the market. If you view it and you still don't like it, I can't show you any better. This is the best.'

'Well, let's go and see it,' I told Mrs Desmond.

The mansion consisted of ten huge bedrooms, each had its own en suite, walk-in closets, and a separate sitting area. There were two large sitting rooms, and a good size dining room that could accommodate 20 people. And then there was a state of the art kitchen which led to a game room with a pool table and a fancy decorated bar to the side. French doors led to the back yard. There was also a large covered patio, an Olympic-size swimming pool, two tennis courts, and garages for eight cars. A short distance from the back of the mansion, there was a bungalow that included two huge bedrooms, each with a private en suite. There was also a kitchen, a dining room, and a living room. The mansion was surrounded by six acres, laid to grass and well maintained. It was also surrounded by an eight-foot brick wall and wired with a sophisticated alarm system.

BJ and I whispered to each other that we both liked the mansion very much, and we agreed to buy it. We returned to the main building, and as we passed by the game room, BJ stopped, looked at the pool table, and with a determined voice, he pointed his finger and said, 'That pool table has to go. We'll have to bring a proper snooker table from England.'

I quickly agreed.

Mrs Desmond told us that the asking price for the mansion was $38 million, but the owner was desperate to sell.

After discussing it privately with BJ, I looked at Mrs Desmond and told her, 'I'll give the owner $30 million, in cash, take it or leave it.'

"Cash" was the magic word. She quickly walked outside and called the owner. It didn't take long before she rushed back to us and said, 'The owner, although he preferred $35 million, will accept your cash offer, only because his divorce became final and he's anxious to leave California.' She also added, 'I know a title company that would complete all the documentation very quickly, and you can get the keys within a week.'

'That's great. By the way, do you know of a good designer who could furnish this mansion in the most luxurious way possible, say within two days after we get the keys, which I assume will be this Friday?'

'Yes, in fact I do. I'll call her this afternoon.'

'One more thing Mrs Desmond. Please make arrangements to have all utilities turned on, and everything in good working order, to include cleaning the pool, by the time we move in.'

'For what you are paying, I will make sure everything is done so you will enjoy your mansion in the best possible way.'

'Thank you Mrs Desmond. Don't forget, when it's all finished, there will be an envelope addressed to you, and only you.'

'Thank you,' she replied, and then left.

At the end of the week Mrs Desmond came to the hotel and gave us the keys to the mansion. 'Everything is done as you asked, and you'll be amazed when you see your new home,' Mrs Desmond said. 'In all the years I've sold houses, I have never seen a mansion as beautiful as this. The designer did a superb job and everything looks very impressive - you will both love it. The designer will send you the bill for all her expenses. I'll leave now, but please call me if you need anything more done. Congratulations on your purchase.'

As she turned to leave, I said, 'Mrs Desmond, don't forget the envelope on the table, I believe it's addressed to you.'

She picked the envelope and walked out smiling and saying, 'Thank you, don't forget to invite me to your first party.'

It was Friday, so we decided to go and shop for new cars. I asked BJ which car he liked, and he replied, 'Well, I've always liked Lexus. What about you, Frank?'

'I also like Lexus, so let's go shopping.'

We went straight to a Lexus dealership. We saw five salesmen talking. One of them hurried towards us. He introduced himself as Joe, and said, 'Do you need help with any car? We have the largest fleet of Lexus cars.'

'Well Joe, this is your lucky day.' He

looked at me, puzzled. I continued, 'Here's what I want, I want four of the best Lexus sports cars, two SUVs, a big truck with an open back to haul big heavy items, and a medium size covered van. They all have to be automatic with powerful engines, top of the line, everything in them, I mean loaded, different colours, and just the best you have. Did you get that Joe?'

Joe was writing down everything I said. He then looked at me and asked, 'Is this a joke or do you mean everything you said. I can't afford to lose my job if this is a joke.'

'No Joe, I'm not joking. Go and call your manager to come to see me. I'll wait here.'

Five minutes later the manager came. I shook his hand, introduced myself, and told him, 'I asked Joe to sell me eight cars, and this young man deserves all the credit. He wrote down exactly what I wanted. It's not a joke. I want Joe to deliver these cars to my house on Monday at noon. I would like you to tell me the total cost, and I'll pay you by credit card. Give me your best deal and I'll be back in an hour to finalise things. And by the way, I would like Joe to get all the credit for this sale, and to get paid the commission. If he doesn't get paid, I'll cancel the order.'

'Yes, sir, Joe will get all the money due to him from this sale, I guarantee it.'

'Thank you,' I said, 'I'll see you in an hour to pay for them. Just make sure I get the cars with all the specs I asked for on Monday, ready to go.'

On Sunday morning, BJ and I moved into our new mansion. As we entered, we were so impressed. We spent the rest of the day exploring our new home. We thought it was super exciting. In the evening we went to a nearby restaurant and enjoyed a great dinner, and then we returned home.

Around noon on Monday, a fleet of eight cars was delivered to our house. Joe was there. I told him to put each of the cars in the garage, and I asked Joe if he was paid for the sale. He said yes, and thanked me for it. 'By the way, Joe, I forgot to ask you, are you married?'

Joe replied, 'Yes sir, to a beautiful girl, my high school sweetheart, and two weeks ago she gave birth to a baby girl. We called her Samantha.'

'That's a beautiful name. You just keep working hard, treat the customers like you treated me, and maybe one day you'll become the manager. I want to thank you, and please give your wife and Samantha our love.'

I then handed Joe an envelope. 'This is for you, don't tell anyone, OK. Take good care of your family. We'll see you sometime.'

'That was very kind of you, Frank,' BJ said.

'It's one way of showing my gratitude, and to show him that customer satisfaction is important in this business. You saw the other guys talking together when we arrived. They couldn't be bothered, but Joe took the initiative to welcome us and help us.'

'Well, BJ, we got the house, it's furnished, we have the cars, and we are ready to start our business. Can we drink to that?'

BJ poured Chivas Regal in two glasses, and we dedicated the drinks to our business.

As we sat down, BJ said, 'All we need now is to look for two girls and a man to work as private investigators on our team. Let's plan to advertise and interview applicants next week.'

'I agree, BJ.'

We advertised for one male and two female private investigators. We thought that would make an adequate team. We received many applicants, and we interviewed them all. Finally we made our selection.

The male investigator we selected was Oliver Montay. He was 27 years old, 6 feet

4 inches tall, muscular, and enjoyed boxing and weight lifting. He was single, and lived in San Francisco. He appeared to have a good sense of humour. To top that, he used to be a chef at one time. He had all the qualities we were looking for. He would also serve as our chef and chauffeur. BJ was glad to have him for the job.

As for the two females, we first selected Rachel Marque, who was 25 years old, 5 feet 6 inches tall, had long blonde hair, and a beautiful figure. She had a lovely smile that showed her perfectly aligned white teeth. Her parents were French, but she was born in Muncie, Indiana. She had a college degree in psychology. She was also a black belt in karate. She was addicted to watching mystery movies and reading mystery novels. Thus her desire to become an investigator.

And the second female we selected was Jackie Johnson, also 25 years old, 5 feet

6 inches tall, with short black hair and a figure that just stood out. She was born in Atlanta, Georgia. She had a college degree in computers and electronics. She was also expert in judo, the art of self-defence. She told us a friend of hers who lived in Los Angeles mentioned the job advertisement to her, so she flew from Atlanta especially for the interview.

Since the three new members of the team were single, they all agreed to move into the mansion. There was plenty of room for everybody. We had our first meeting as a team, and to my gratification the five of us appeared to meld well. As time went by, we got to know each other very well.

We became one big family.

#

My life was still flashing in front of me, remembering all my past, when I felt someone shaking me. I opened my eyes, and saw BJ staring at me.

'Are you OK, Frank?' he asked.

'Yes BJ, I'm fine. I was just day dreaming.'

'I suggest we better go inside because it's getting hot and you're beginning to sweat. You don't want to be barbecued, do you?' BJ asked me.

'No, not today, BJ. Let's go inside.'

CHAPTER SIX

We had been in the private investigation business for about a year. We had some exciting cases, and most of our customers were rich residents who lived in Los Angeles, Beverly Hills, and Hollywood. We were sometimes hired by desperate housewives who wanted us to track their husbands, or hired by husbands who suspected their wives were cheating on them. They all demanded actual photos as their proof.

We were also hired to find runaway teenagers who were hooked on drugs and lived on the streets or who squatted in derelict buildings. Since our business was new we learned a lot from the experience, which we needed. And we enjoyed it.

However, we were then placed in a situation that tested our abilities as capable private investigators. A wealthy movie director, who lived in San Diego, asked us to rescue his eight year old son, called Jason, who had been kidnapped and was being held for ransom. The movie director did not want the police to get involved because he was afraid his son would be killed. That's what the kidnappers told him - pay the ransom or we kill your son. The director only wanted us to carry the ransom money, give it to the kidnappers, and bring his son back safely.

We accepted the job. However, when our team gathered to discuss a plan, we realised there was no guarantee that we would find the boy alive, because if he had seen the kidnappers, they would definitely kill him as soon as they get hold of the ransom money.

This was a sensitive and dangerous situation; we couldn't take a chance. So, we decided it would be better to inform the San

Diego Police Department about what was going on and solicit their assistance. The Chief of Police, Jim Shannon, agreed to help us. We did not tell the movie director about our plan to get the police involved.

Our plan went well. Jackie hid in the back seat of the car. Oliver was the driver, and I was to carry the bag of money and go to an old abandoned warehouse outside the city to deliver it. Rachel was to stay with Jim and his officers.

Oliver drove to the warehouse, and we waited for the kidnappers. They arrived in a van. The driver got out of the van, took a good look around the warehouse and walked half way towards me. He had a hood covering his face. He asked for the money.

'I need to see the kid first, then I'll give you the money,' I said. The kidnapper was anxious to get hold of the money. He looked around, and then waved his hand to his partner to show us the boy.

After I saw the boy, I went to the car and brought the bag of money. I walked towards the kidnapper, opened the bag, and showed him the money. He was full of smiles. I looked at him and said, 'You let the boy walk to me, then I will hand you the money, and we will leave. We don't care about the money, it's yours. We only want the boy alive; we are just the messengers.'

He looked at me and appeared to be thinking. Then he turned and waved again to his partner who let the boy walk towards me. As soon as the boy came up to me, I handed the bag of money to the kidnapper who started to scream with joy as he ran to the van with the bag while the boy and I rushed to the car, and Oliver drove off as fast as he could.

The kidnappers weren't able to drive far, as a number of police cars appeared, surrounded the van, and arrested them.

This case made the news headlines; breaking news on television and radio, and front page coverage in all California newspapers. We needed the publicity. At last we had done something big and we were proud of it, and of course, we learned from it. It also helped us build a good relationship with the San Diego Police Department.

Since we ran the business from the mansion, we had plenty of free time, and each of us had a hobby. I enjoyed swimming, watercolour painting, and listening to songs of the 60's and 70's. I also enjoyed watching old black and white movies.

BJ and Oliver lifted weights and worked out daily. BJ taught Oliver how to play snooker, which Oliver eventually mastered. Since Oliver enjoyed cooking, he often prepared gourmet dishes that he created. I suggested that he publish his own cookery book. He refused and said he didn't want someone to mess with his ingredients.

Rachel and Jackie jogged five miles every day, played tennis, practiced karate and judo, and did a lot of swimming. Some days they went shopping and had a fun day out.

One warm sunny day, BJ and I played tennis, and then swam for a while. We were getting tired, so we each had a Chivas Regal on the rocks and lay back on the deck chair by the pool. As we rested, BJ turned to me and said to me, 'Isn't this beautiful, doing something you enjoy, with a group of people you love, who are friends for life. I'm so happy.'

BJ looked at me, and saw I was quiet, so he asked me, 'Frank, were you ever in love, I mean really deeply in love?'

That question caught me by surprise. Yes, I was in love once, some years ago. But I kept it a secret because it brought back wonderful and sad memories. However, I didn't want to ignore BJ's question.

'Yes BJ, I was deeply in love once, but I prefer not to talk about it.'

'Frank, I can't stand seeing you unhappy. For a long time I've noticed that something has been bothering you. You don't have a girlfriend, and many times I see you sit alone with a drink in your hand and you appear to be day dreaming, like you are on another planet.'

'BJ, I have my reasons. Maybe one day the right girl will come along. Right now I don't want to talk about it.'

'When will you talk about it, Frank, when you get old? Look, we're like brothers, and we should look after each other. I'm worried about you. So please tell me all about it. Maybe I can help you.'

I heard what BJ said. He was probably right, but I didn't want to go through the pain of uncovering such a sad chapter of my life.

After a pause, BJ said in a demanding voice, 'Listen Frank, you must tell me now and get it off your chest, or - or I'll throw you in the swimming pool.'

I turned around and looked at BJ. He gave me his usual big smile, showing me his white teeth. He always did that whenever he wanted to get something out of me.

I thought about it for a minute, and then said to BJ, 'You're my best friend BJ, and if I had to get it off my chest, it would only be to you.'

'I'm all ears Frank, so tell me all about it, but don't skip the sexy part. Let me get comfortable. Oh, by the way, should I get some popcorn and beer?'

I smiled, and reluctantly started telling BJ all about my true love and only love.

CHAPTER SEVEN

During my last year at the University of Wales in Bangor, and in order to complete my graduate requirements, I had to write a thesis about the history of Ancient Egypt. To accurately write such a thesis I decided to go to Cairo and do my research. I had heard and read so much about the beauty of Egypt that I thought it would be an excellent opportunity to do my research and at the same time travel around Egypt. The university gave me permission to go.

My mother was worried about my safety, being alone in Cairo. She heard so much about troubles in the Middle East, she thought it would be the same in Cairo. I explained to her that Cairo was a safe place because special Egyptian secret police were spread all around Cairo to protect the people and the tourists.

My mother felt I would be safer if I stayed in one of the best hotels in Cairo and advised me never to speak to strangers. I promised her I would be very careful. How could anyone deny her; she always worried about me and tried to protect me - I was her only son.

The flight from London to Cairo took about four and half hours. I had a first class seat, and the British Airways crew provided excellent service. On arrival I went through passport control and then retrieved my luggage. On my way out I saw a well-dressed Egyptian man holding a poster with my name on it. I walked to him and told him that I was Frank Mackintosh. He smiled, and in fairly good English, he said, 'My name is Ahmed, and I have a limousine to take you to your hotel.'

'How did you know I was coming? I did not reserve a limousine.'

'Yes sir, I know. The reservation was made by a Mrs Mackintosh.'

What can I say, mothers will always be mothers, especially my mother.

'Thank you, Ahmed. You can take me to the hotel now.'

The drive from the airport to the hotel was a hectic one; I could see why it was important to always rent a car with a driver in Egypt, as they knew how to handle driving situations in Cairo. I felt sorry for Ahmed. But finally we made it to the hotel. The hotel was huge and modern. It was situated alongside the Nile.

As soon as I got out of the limousine, Ahmed gave me his business card, and with a smile he said, 'Mr Mackintosh, if you ever need to go anywhere, just call me and I will be happy to take you. I know Cairo very well. And next time, I will have a smaller luxury car, and not a huge limousine.'

'Thank you Ahmed. I will do that. And by the way, call me Frank, OK?'

The hotel was one of the largest and most modern hotels in Cairo. My room was on the 12th floor overlooking the Nile. It was large, had a king size bed, a separate sitting area with a couch and two chairs, and a fully stocked bar. There was a basket of fruit in the middle of the table, and a sign by the fridge that read, "Please drink bottled water". I was impressed by the cleanliness of the room. It seemed that everything was geared towards making sure the guests were comfortable and happy.

After I unpacked I had a shower and rested for about an hour. I then decided to go downstairs and check the facilities. There were some fancy retail shops, a coffee shop, a bar surrounded by tables, which led me to a huge restaurant and a good size dance floor. The manager noticed my fascination with the place. He approached me and introduced himself as Fahed, and said, 'You seem excited by the decor. Wait until you go to the top floor, you will be amazed by what you will see there. The restaurant is the best in Egypt. Food is exotic, and entertainment is out of this world. There is music, variety shows every night, belly dancers with Egyptian singers, and much more.'

'I assume you know where I will have dinner tonight. Please make me a reservation for, say, for 8 o'clock. Thank you.'

When I went to the top floor, I realised the manager was right. There was a huge fantastic dining room, with a large dance floor in the middle, and a stage for the band. And if guests wanted to sit quietly, have a drink, and chat, then there was a room nearby especially for them, with soft music playing all the time. I was impressed. I had a wonderful dinner, one to remember.

Two days later I went to the History Department in Cairo University. I met with the professor who I had been referred to. He showed me the University Library and told me that if I needed anything, all I had to do was ask him.

The research kept me busy every day, from Sunday to Thursday, as the weekend in Egypt started on Fridays. The professors at the University were very helpful, giving me advice and direction so that I could write a good thesis. They were proud of their history and they wanted the world to know about it.

I rested on Fridays. Fridays is a holy day in Egypt and all Muslim countries, just like Sundays in Christian countries. Fridays in Egypt is a day of rest and prayers. It is also a family day, where Egyptians take their children to the zoo, parks, and end up with late dinners. Restaurants are open until the early hours of the morning.

On Fridays I always went to Khan-el-Khalili, the biggest market in the old district of Cairo. It was full of twisting alleys, with shops that sold jewellery, gold and silver, brass, and handmade leather products. Papyrus paintings, framed and unframed, and other crafts were also sold. Khan-el-Khalili is a popular place for tourists. It is always crowded, and you could easily get cheap bargains:18 or 24 carat gold rings, bracelets, or any other jewellery, as the jewellers make you anything you desire. I was told to always bargain, never pay what was asked.

A professor at Cairo University told me that I should look for a jeweller by the name of Gallal because he had the best quality gold and silver, and was the best jeweller, and the cheapest, at Khan-el-Khalili.

The following Friday I called Ahmed and asked him to take me to Khan-el-Khalili. Ahmed knew where Gallal's shop was, so he escorted me there.

I introduced myself to Gallal, and told him that a professor at Cairo University recommended that I see him. Gallal knew the professor. Gallal was a big man, about 6 feet tall, muscular, and always wore gallabia (a long robe). He always smiled, and looked like a friendly type, easy to get along with.

Gallal and I hit it off right from the beginning. He spoke good English, was married to an Irish girl, and had a two-year old boy called Ali. The tradition in Egypt is that if your first child is a boy, the father will be called "father of his son". Because his son was called Ali, then Gallal was called "Abu Ali", that meant "Father of Ali".

I enjoyed Gallal's company so much that I started to go to his shop every Friday and spend the day with him. I often helped him sell jewellery to tourists. I always had dinner in his house on Friday nights. His wife cooked some delicious Irish food. As time went by, Gallal taught me the Arabic language, and I soon became good at it.

One Friday morning I went to his shop as usual. When I entered the shop, Gallal was busy talking to a girl. He saw me come in so he waved at me. At that moment the girl he was talking to turned around. And our eyes met. If you believe in love at first sight, that was it. It was like magic. She was the most beautiful girl I had ever seen. She was about 5 feet 6 inches tall, brunette, with gorgeous blue eyes. She was dressed in tight blue jeans and a short sleeve top which showed her well-shaped body. We kept staring at each other, our eyes just focussing on each other. We didn't pay attention to anything else around us. My heart was pounding fast, and I had butterflies in my stomach. I smiled, and she smiled back at me.

Gallal noticed what was happening, so he coughed to attract our attention. He called me to him and introduced us.

'Frank, this is Carla. She is an American visiting Cairo for two weeks' vacation.' Then he looked at Carla and said, 'Carla, this is Frank. He is a Welshman trying to complete his graduate thesis here in Cairo.'

I gently took her hand, and kept holding it, saying, 'It's a pleasure to meet you, Carla. I hope you're enjoying your vacation. Are you visiting alone?'

'Yes, I'm enjoying my vacation, and yes, I am visiting alone,' Carla answered while smiling, and then added, 'I assume you are very busy working on your thesis.'

'I take a break once in a while. It gets boring sometimes, so I visit my friend Gallal,' I commented.

Throughout our conversation, we continued to look at each other. She had beautiful eyes, and her lips - I can't even describe them. I was wondering if she felt the same way I did.

Gallal had planned to take me out to lunch that day, but after he noticed the sparks between me and Carla, he told us that he had wanted to take me to lunch but he couldn't now because he was expecting an important customer from Paris. I was sure he made that up.

'I'm sorry about that, Frank. But I have a suggestion. Why don't you take Carla for lunch?' Gallal asked.

I turned to Carla and asked her, 'Would you like to have lunch with a Welshman?'

'I'd love that,' Carla answered.

'Well, Gallal, its settled. You meet your French customer, and Carla and will go to lunch.'

I'm normally a shy person, but I just couldn't miss this opportunity, and the words just came out of my mouth. My heart was beating hard and my stomach was churning. I didn't know how I was going to behave because I had never been in the company of such a beautiful girl, especially since we had only just met.

Gallal looked at me and smiled as we left the shop.

Ahmed was waiting for me, so I asked him to take us to a good restaurant somewhere along the Nile. While in the car, I found myself holding Carla's hand. I don't know how it happened, it was a sudden urge to touch her. Soon I felt a responding pressure from her hand. She must have felt the same way because her hand was warm.

Ahmed took us to the Swiss Air Restaurant, a fancy and popular European restaurant overlooking the Nile. The manager welcomed us as soon as we entered. He guided us to a secluded table. Ahmed must have brought many tourists to this restaurant, and I am sure the manager always gave him a tip.

I told Ahmed that I would not need him for the rest of the day, but would need him tomorrow. My hotel was close to the restaurant.

As we sat down, we didn't say a word; we just stared at each other. I couldn't take it anymore. I wanted to be strong and let my feelings do the talking. I leaned forward and held Carla's hands, and said in a soft voice, 'Carla, I don't know how to say this. Please forgive me for being so forward - what I am trying to say is that you are the most beautiful girl I have ever met. From the moment I saw you I had this strong desire to hold you close to me and kiss you.'

I was meeting her gaze when she said, 'I also felt the same way Frank. I felt a sudden attraction and desire that has never happened to me before. My heart beats fast when I look at you, like right now, and I too want to hold you and kiss you.'

I was about to kiss her hands, when the waiter interrupted us.

We both ordered the restaurant's special mixed salad with crumbled feta cheese and slices of chicken breast. We had a bottle of white wine, and for dessert we had small slices of baklavas.

When we finished eating, we left the restaurant and walked along the Nile, holding hands. We were boiling with passion and desire for love. Since my hotel was close by, we decided to go there. I couldn't get to the 12th floor fast enough. As soon as we entered my room, and without turning on the lights, we gently hugged and kissed. I could never forget that first kiss; it must have lasted over three minutes. Our lips and tongues were getting warmer and warmer, and we couldn't control ourselves.

We quickly but gently undressed each other and we made love. We did not leave the room for the rest of the night, and it was a long beautiful night; we made love over and over. I kissed every part of her body, and we did everything imaginable to please each other. We simply gave ourselves to each other. There was no end to our energy and desire for love. We finally fell asleep hugging each other - and totally naked.

I could never forget that first night; we were full of love. There I was with a beautiful girl I had met few hours earlier. I didn't know anything about her, and she didn't know anything about me, yet we had this strong mutual attraction and desire for each other. We forgot the world around us and were engulfed with passionate love.

It was about five o'clock in the morning when I was awakened by the voice of the

Muezzin reciting Koran prayers from the top of a nearby mosque, calling on Muslims to pray. I liked his voice, and I listened to him every morning.

I got out of bed, naked, put on a robe, and went out on the balcony to listen to the Muezzin. I also thought about my relationship with Carla. Was that how Father and Mother met and fell in love?

When the Muezzin finished his prayer call, I remained on the balcony admiring the beauty of the Nile and the sunrise. I could see the fishermen unloading their fish helped by their young children. The University Bridge was crowded with donkeys pulling carts loaded with fruit and vegetables heading to the market. I felt sorry for the donkeys pulling such heavy loads.

At around 7 o'clock when I went back into the bedroom, I called room service and ordered breakfast. I then sat on the bed watching Carla sleeping. I was admiring her beauty when she opened her eyes. She smiled at me, and without saying a word she held her arms and pulled me to her and kissed me.

'Frank, I had a wonderful time last night. You know how to please a girl. I want it to be like this every night. I want to feel your naked body. I want to kiss you all over, and make love.'

I hugged her and kissed her passionately, getting warm for another love session when I heard a knock on the door. 'Breakfast is here, you must be hungry.'

We had breakfast, and then we took a shower together - a long shower. Afterwards I suggested we tour Cairo, saying, 'Cairo is a fascinating city, you must see it.'

As we were about to leave the room, I put my arms around Carla, and said, 'Carla, you are a wonderful girl, and I love those beautiful blue eyes of yours. I will always remember and treasure our love last night.'

Carla liked that. She smiled, pulled me to her, and we enjoyed a long passionate kiss. Then we left for our tour.

CHAPTER EIGHT

The weather was always good by the Nile: sunny and warm with a light breeze. I wanted to take Carla for a ride on a Felucca (an Egyptian sailing boat). Many of the Feluccas were parked, marked "For Hire". One of the Felucca owners, an older man, saw us coming so he rushed to us and in broken English, he told us that he would take us on a two-hour ride for 10 Egyptian pounds. I thought that was cheap, so I gave him 20 pounds. He was thrilled and thanked me. He seated us on a cushioned bench in the front of the Felucca. I sat behind Carla with my arms around her waist, and she rested her back on my chest. Carla was afraid at first when we set sail, but shortly afterwards she was relaxed.

The wind was blowing Carla's hair on my face. I would kiss her neck every now and then, and at times she would pull me gently and kiss me on the lips; every kiss was full of love and desire. The ride was great; we enjoyed every minute.

After we got off the boat, we decided that since we would be together all the time, it would be better if Carla checked out of her hotel and moved in with me. That afternoon, I called Ahmed. He drove us to Carla's hotel where she checked out, and then moved to my hotel. I was glad to have Ahmed drive us around and help us with the luggage. After Carla settled, Ahmed took us to the pyramids, the sphinx at Giza, the Egyptian Museum which contained some of the most fascinating artifacts from ancient Egypt, and the tombs of the ancient Egyptian kings. The next day we took a cruise to Aswan Dam and Luxor. One day I asked Ahmed to take us to Alexandria, a city in the north tip of Egypt on the Mediterranean Sea. He was happy to take us, so he picked us up at 9 o'clock in the morning. We spent the day in Alexandria swimming, playfully chasing each other, and having fun. Along the beach there were small restaurants which served fresh fish and large shrimps, cooked in front of us. They were perfectly spiced, simply delicious. We ate so much that we had to lay on the beach and rest. It was getting late, so Ahmed took us back to the hotel.

When we returned to the hotel, we were again boiling with desire for love. We had a shower, and ended in bed for another night of passionate love.

The following day we woke up around noon. We were exhausted from the day and night before; we needed the rest. We hadn't seen Gallal for two days, so I gave him a call. He invited us for dinner. We agreed. I called Ahmed to pick us at 5 pm.

Gallal was waiting for us. His wife did not come; she had prior engagement. He hugged both of us then we walked with him to his favourite restaurant. I liked the restaurant too: everything was cooked on an open fire in front of us. There were plenty of small plates of appetisers. The dinner was delicious, but we had no space for dessert.

'I think if we kept eating like this, we will end up putting on lots of weight,' I whispered to Carla.

'I don't think so. You probably lose it at night,' Carla said, smiling.

I looked at Carla and smiled in return.

While eating dinner, I had a private chat with Gallal without Carla knowing. I asked Gallal if he would make me a 24ct gold heart shaped pendant. It needed to be large because I wanted to put a picture of myself and Carla together. I also asked him for a thick 24ct 18 inch gold chain. He agreed to do it. He said it would be done in few days' time. One thing about Gallal: he is loyal to his friends, and you can always depend on him.

We thanked Gallal for the wonderful and delicious dinner. Ahmed was there to take us to the hotel.

In the car I asked Ahmed if the Sound and Light Show was still shown by the sphinx and pyramids.

'Yes, it normally starts when it gets dark, so you never know the exact time. Do you want to see it now? I don't think it's started yet.'

I asked Carla if she wanted to see it, and she agreed. We arrived there just in time to see it from the beginning. The place was full of tourists. As soon as we sat down, the lights in the area were turned off. We were in complete darkness, and there was not a sound from the crowd. The show started with soft ancient Egyptian music and soon a man appeared with lights focused on him only. The man was narrating the history of the sphinx and the pyramids. The music followed the narrator, and it was loud at times, and then it became softer. At the same time, the narrator was dramatized through the use of light, which appeared in different sections of the sphinx and the pyramids. We enjoyed the show very much, but we were getting tired, so Ahmed drove us to the hotel.

The next day I woke up around noon. Carla was still in bed, she laid there naked looking sexier than ever. She opened her eyes and invited me back to bed. I was tempted.

'I'd love to darling, but today I want to take you somewhere exciting, and we are going to need our strength; it will be a long afternoon and night.'

I called room service and ordered lunch. We took a shower and dressed. After we had lunch, I asked Carla, 'How would you like to go horseback riding in the desert this afternoon?'

'I'd love to,' she replied, but with an anxious tone to her voice.

It was 3 o'clock when Ahmed called and said he was downstairs. Ahmed drove us to the pyramids. We held hands as we strolled around the pyramids. The place was packed with tourists. We came across a sign that said, "Horses for Rent". I asked the owner if we could rent two horses for the afternoon. I asked to pay him, but he said, 'You can pay me when you bring them back.'

'Do you believe people bring the horses back? What if they run away with them?' I asked him.

'Don't worry, these horses are trained. They know their home. If they don't come back, they'll just leave you wherever you are, and they come back to me.'

He saddled two horses, and gave us two zamzamias (leather pouches filled with ice cold water). 'You will need these, they contain cold water just in case you get hot and thirsty, which I am sure you will.'

Just before we headed out, I told Ahmed not to wait for us because we might be late.

The sun was disappearing as we rode out slowly. Carla knew how to ride very well. Soon we were chasing each other, and we stopped often and kissed. We were getting thirsty, so we stopped and drank from the zamzamias. Carla found it difficult to use hers, and water kept splashing on her face and chest. I showed her how to use it properly. The horse owner was right; the zamzamias kept the water cold. It started to get dark, so we decided to go back.

It was around 7 o'clock when we returned to the horse stable. After I paid for use of the horses, I asked Carla what she wanted to eat for supper. The owner heard us, so he approached us and said, 'I heard you say you want to go to a nice place for supper. Well, I know this popular place about two miles from here, not in town but in the desert. Every night they have a dinner party. They serve authentic Egyptian food in a huge tent. There is music, dancing and lots of entertainment. It's very popular with tourists. But there is a problem; to get there you have to ride a camel.'

I asked Carla, 'How would you like to ride a camel for about two miles.'

'I don't mind, as long as it doesn't kick me.'

I looked at the owner and said, 'Go ahead and add us to your list.'

The owner then said, 'The cost of riding the camel roundtrip (he looked at us and smiled) plus the dinner, music and entertainment is 200 Egyptian pounds for both of you. Is that OK?'

I agreed and paid him in advance.

'Thank you. Here are two clean towels to clean yourselves before we go, say in another half hour.'

Carla and I washed our hands and faces and dusted the sand from our clothes and shoes. We looked better.

'This should be fun. I like new adventures. I assume this is the surprise you were telling me about,' Carla commented.

The camel ride was a lot of fun. It took about half an hour and we laughed all the way . The party was in a huge tent, the size of a basketball court, and carpeted. It was full of tourists. Guests were seated around the tent, on soft large pads, on carpets. In the corner of the tent, there were five musicians playing Egyptian music. The dinner was about to be served.

As usual, the Egyptians like to start with a variety of appetisers consisting of feta cheese, various cheeses, black and green olives, cucumbers, humous , basturma (cured spiced lamb tenderloin), pickles, tomatoes, rice, and much more. The main dishes consisted of lamb and chicken kebab (marinated and spiced), kofta, baked and fried fish and chicken, stuffed grape leaves, various casseroles and much more. As for dessert, there were a variety of cakes, fresh fruit, baklava, and more. There were bottles of cold water, beer, whisky, soft drinks, hot tea, and espresso coffee. There was enough to feed an army. Everything was delicious.

Throughout dinner there was Egyptian music and singing and belly dancing. A belly dancer came near us as the music stopped and a host introduced her as a famous Egyptian belly dancer called Samia.

As soon as the host finished the introduction, the loud sounds of drums started the music, and Samia started to dance, belly dancing. Everybody in the tent started to clap. Her belly systematically moved with the music. We had never seen such a professional belly dancer. We started to clap and joined in the celebration.

After showing us her talent and keeping us entertained, Samia slowed down, walked around and stopped in front of Carla. She pointed at Carla and asked her to join in the dancing. Carla looked at me, shy and hesitant.

'Go ahead, it will be fun.' I said.

Carla stood up and Samia tied a scarf around her hips. Samia started to belly dance, and Carla imitated her movements. To my surprise, Carla proved to be an apt pupil. She seemed to enjoy belly dancing. I thought Carla looked sexy. When Samia and Carla finished dancing the audience stood up and clapped. Samia took her scarf off Carla's hips and gave it to her, saying, 'You did well, keep this scarf as a souvenir.'

That was a most wonderful evening. We were both exhausted by the time we returned to the hotel. We had a shower and then I opened a bottle of champagne, poured two glasses and sat in the balcony. After few minutes Carla went into the room, and soon after she called me. When I went into the room, Carla was standing by the bed, completely naked except for the scarf Samia gave her. It was tied to her hips, and she started to belly dance. Carla looked gorgeous and sexy. After watching her dance for a minute, I couldn't resist it any more. I dropped my robe and we hugged and kissed passionately, and we both laid on the bed naked and made love.

'Did you like my dancing, darling?'

'I loved it, you are becoming good at it.'

There were nights when we just sat on the balcony, and watched the fishing boats and Feluccas sail by as we listened to the songs of Baccara, and drank champagne. We made love every chance we could; the physical attraction between us was so intense, it was like a giant bush fire out of control.

During the two weeks we spent together, we didn't discuss our personal life. All we cared about was our unique relationship that developed in such a short time, and the love we had for each other. Carla only knew that I was born in Rhyl, that I attended the University of Wales in Bangor, and that I was in Cairo to write my graduate thesis. As for her, she was born in Milwaukee, Wisconsin, and was presently working as a dental assistant.

Deep in my heart I knew I was in love with Carla, and that she felt the same way towards me. We got along very well, and we enjoyed each other's company. We also enjoyed our lovemaking; there was no end to it. It was always exciting, as if we were making love for the first time.

CHAPTER NINE

The night before Carla was due to fly back to America, we had a candlelight dinner at the Swiss Air Restaurant. For the first time since we met, we were both lost for words. The dinner was superb.

We left the restaurant and walked along the Nile towards the hotel. In the room, a bottle of champagne was waiting for us, and Baccara was singing in the background. We sat on the balcony, holding each other tightly. We were both quiet because we knew it was time to part. Carla sat on my lap, hugged me, and with wet eyes she said, 'Why did it have to end? I am going to miss you, Frank. I love you so much, and I wish I could stay with you.'

'Stay with me, don't go.'

'I have to go Frank. I have some important things I need to do. As soon as you graduate, we could meet in America.'

'I love you Blue Eyes. I will never forget you and those wonderful days and nights we spent together.'

Carla put her lips close to mine, and with tears falling down her cheeks, we kissed. I carried her to bed and we made love once again.

That night I couldn't sleep. I kept thinking about Carla being away, and how much I would miss her. I got out of bed, covered Carla, and went to the balcony. I wanted to give Carla something to remember me by. I already had the pendant and chain that Gallal made for her, but I wanted to give her something original. After thinking about it I decided to write her a special poem, just for her. I will always remember that poem. I called it "My Blue Eyes".

We were strangers when we met
    At the top of Gallal's nest.
I gazed at your Blue Eyes
    And I knew that you were mine.
We left the Khan hand-in-hand
    With feelings unique and grand.
Never before have I felt like this
    It became stronger from the first kiss.
A Felucca ride, dinner by candlelight
    All our worries were put aside.
Nothing stopped our desire
    We were like a ball of fire.
Those were unforgettable days
    Full of love and emotions.
My Blue Eyes, I will always remember you
    And I will always love you.

I just finished taking a shower when Carla woke up. I could tell she was reading the poem, and before I knew it, she came behind me and hugged me while kissing my back.

'That's a wonderful poem darling, original too. And the pendant, it's beautiful, too. I will always treasure both of your gifts.'

She turned me around and kissed me. Our hearts were beating hard as we returned to bed and made love. It felt like we were making love for the first time. Then we laid naked staring at each other. After few minutes, Carla turned me on my back and sat on top of me. She kissed me, and said, 'Frank, I love you very much. You are my only true love. I have never felt like this before. No man will ever take your place.'

'And no woman will ever take your place darling. I promise you.'

After a brief pause I pulled Carla closer to me and we kissed and kissed. But time was getting short. Carla took a shower and got dressed. Ahmed was waiting for us outside. We loaded the luggage, and headed to the airport. At the airport, Ahmed looked sad.

He looked at Carla and said, 'I am sorry to see you go Miss Carla. You are a wonderful lady. I hope to see you again.'

Carla looked at Ahmed and hugged him, saying, 'Thank you for everything you did. I am sure we will meet again. Take care of Frank.'

After checking in the luggage, Carla had about half an hour before boarding her flight. I was tense and shaking. We walked to a secluded spot in the departure lounge, and we hugged and kissed; I didn't want to let her go.

I was sad when I told Carla, 'Carla, I love you with all my heart and I want to marry you. You are mine and I want us to be together, forever.' My tears kept flowing.

Carla wiped my tears with her hand, and said, 'Frank, no matter what the future holds, I will always love you and you will always be on my mind.' Gently kissing me, and then holding my face with her two hands, she continued, 'I had the best time of my life. Frank. I will miss you, and I will miss your lips, your body, and your love.'

Carla started to cry when we heard the voice of the speaker announcing the boarding of her flight. We hugged for the last time and kissed. Carla kept looking back at me as she walked towards the boarding gate, and then she vanished. I ran to the window overlooking her flight, and I kept waving even as the flight took off.

My stomach was tearing apart; I didn't want Carla to leave. I wanted her to stay with me forever. I couldn't stop crying as I slowly went down on my knees. I was crying like a baby hungry for food, but I was hungry for Carla.

I was kneeling down with my hands on my face when someone touched my shoulder. I looked up and saw an old

Egyptian woman. She must have been over 80 years old. She spoke to me in Arabic, and said while pointing up with her right hand finger, 'Don't cry, my son, God will bring you together again.' She must have seen what happened and wanted to make me feel better.

'You are kind, and thank you for your encouraging words,' I told her in broken Arabic. She slowly walked away with a smile on her face.

I didn't say a word to Ahmed as he drove me back to the hotel. At the hotel, Ahmed told me, 'I know how much you and Miss Carla love each other. I can see it. I will pray to Allah (God) that you see her again, and have a family with her.'

'Thank you Ahmed. I will call you tomorrow, if I feel good.'

Back in my hotel room, I felt like I was in the middle of the desert with no one around.

I was lonely. Carla was not here with me. I took a bottle of whiskey, sat on the balcony, and listened to the voices of Baccara. I kept thinking of Carla and the time we spent together. I loved her so much. I must have fallen asleep on the balcony because the next thing I heard was the voice of the Muezzin praying from top of the mosque.

I couldn't get Carla out of my mind. She was with me everywhere, even while working on my thesis. I found it difficult to concentrate, but I finally finished the thesis.

Before leaving Cairo I went to see Gallal. He was happy to see me. After he closed his shop, we walked to his house where his wife had dinner ready. After dinner I told Gallal about my relationship with Carla, and how much I missed her.

'Listen Frank. One thing I must tell you. Fate brought you together, and fate will bring you together again.'

'Gallal, you have truly been a good friend, and I thank you for all you have done for me. I wish I could repay you.'

'You don't owe me anything Frank, just have faith and you will meet Carla again. Make sure you come back and see me - with Carla.'

'I will. I promise.'

As I left, I hugged Gallal, his wife, and son Ali. I felt Gallal's heart beating as we hugged. I knew he would miss me just as I would miss him.

At the conclusion of my story, I said to BJ, 'Cairo will always be a special place for me, BJ, not only because of its beauty, but because it was the place where Carla and I met. The memory of our Felucca ride, the horseback trip in the desert, and her belly dancing will always remain with me. And not to forget the magic we shared in bed.'

When I returned to Rhyl I spent few days

with my mother before returning to the university.

My professor was impressed with my thesis. He gave me the highest mark, and I graduated with honours.

I tried to call Carla in Milwaukee several times after I returned, but without success. I called the city telephone operators for assistance but they kept telling me that the telephone number I wanted was disconnected. They told me the party with that number must have left town. I was not about to give up.

I told BJ, 'You see, BJ, when you asked me why I acted the way I did, it was because I am still deeply in love with Carla, and I don't know if I will ever forget her. I just hope nothing has happened to her and that she is doing well.'

BJ looked at me, and in his usual sympathetic voice he said, 'I feel for you

Frank. You really love this Carla. What if you never find her, what would you do? Six years is a long time.'

Lifting my glass of whisky and turning to BJ, I said, 'Thanks for worrying about me BJ. Maybe Gallal was right. Maybe fate will bring us together again, one day.'

I was thinking about Carla as I laid my head back on the chair and closed my eyes. A few minutes after I closed my eyes, Oliver approached me and told me that someone who looked like a new client, wanted to see me, and asked for me by name.

'Well, I should go and see this client then.'

As I entered the living room and was about to speak, the client waiting to see me turned around and faced me. I stood still in shock. The client in front of me was Carla, my lost true love.

CHAPTER TEN

I was in shock! I slowly walked towards her. I wanted to hold her and kiss her. She was still as beautiful as ever, and I loved her more than anything in the world.

I didn't have to wait long. Carla ran to me and we hugged and kissed. It was absolutely thrilling to hold Carla and kiss her again. Kissing her cheeks, forehead, and lips while pushing her hair back, I said, 'I missed you darling, my beautiful Blue Eyes.'

'I missed you too, Frank,' Carla whispered in a desirable tone while hugging me tighter, 'and I missed your lips. Kiss me again.' We continued to kiss passionately. Then Carla looked at me and said, 'I feel awful Frank, coming to you after all these years.' I could see tears on her cheeks.

Brushing her tears while kissing her, I said, 'Carla, I am very happy you came. I have thought of you every day since you left Cairo. I tried to contact you many times but it was as if you vanished.' I paused, and then looking at her blue eyes, 'Oh Carla, I love you so much. Did you know -?'

Gently putting her fingers on my lips, Carla interrupted me, 'Yes, I know how you must have felt because I felt the same way. Frank, you must know that I have never stopped loving you. Those days in Cairo were the best days of my life, days I will never forget.'

Carla hugged me tight and we kissed again; the same passionate kisses we shared in Cairo. As I seated her on the couch, she said, 'I couldn't tell you anything about myself because I didn't want to spoil our relationship, and those wonderful times we spent together. Every time we made love, it was the greatest love I ever enjoyed. I felt as if I was on a different planet. I didn't want to lose you.'

'But why didn't you keep in touch? You knew how much you meant to me. I was going out of my mind. I love you Carla.'

'I was planning to call you, but many things happened that stopped me.' Carla hesitated and then continued, 'I didn't want to hurt you, Frank, by telling you that I was married.'

'You're married?' I said while looking at Carla with disbelief.

In a sad voice, Carla said, 'Yes, unfortunately I was married. But the marriage was never consummated. I often wished my situation was different because I love you Frank, with all my heart. Do you remember the last time we made love? That was about six years ago. It was the last time I made love to anyone. I have never made love with my husband.'

'I believe you Carla. I also have to tell you that you are the only girl I have made love to.'

My love for Carla was so strong that I did not care whether she was married or not. I believed what she told me. What mattered now was that she was back with me.

As we hugged, Carla started to cry, and I suspected that there was something she did not want to tell me.

I handed Carla a glass of water, and asked her, 'What's wrong Carla, what is bothering you?'

It took Carla few seconds to settle down, and then she said, 'I live in San Diego now. I saw you on television a few months ago when you were interviewed about your team's rescue of the kidnapped boy. I was so happy to find out that you were not far away. I wanted to come and see you right away, but it was difficult. So many things have happened in the past few months.'

'What kind of things?' I asked curiously.

'Before I tell you that, I want you to know one thing,' Carla paused for few seconds, and then continued, 'my parents and my in-laws were neighbours for many years. They were very close friends, and they were both from very rich families. They had a son who I went to school with, and we were friends, but only friends. Both parents arranged for us to marry when we got older. Soon after graduation, the families made plans for the wedding, although my parents knew I did not love him. They pressured me to marry him. My father always believed that rich people must marry rich people. He believed in keeping it in the family.'

Carla had a sip of water and then continued, 'The first few months after the wedding, I noticed my husband tried to avoid making love to me all the time. One day I questioned him because I wanted to have children. He came out with the reason right away, and told me that while in college he caught some sort of disease which ultimately led to him not being able to have children. I was furious, and asked him why he didn't tell me, because had I known that, I would have gone to court and got a divorce rather than live without children. He apologised, and said he assumed I knew about it. So he spent most of his time studying, trying to be a doctor, and I stayed home lonely. He finally became a famous research doctor, and travelled around the world, especially Africa. In his last 30-day trip to Zaire, I decided to take a vacation and go to Cairo. What a wonderful decision that turned out to be. I met the most handsome man in the world, and falling in love with him was the most wonderful thing that happened to me. It woke me up from a nightmare marriage. I meant every word, Frank. From the moment I met you at Gallal's shop I fell in love with you. I didn't realise that sex and love were so beautiful - I loved every minute of it Frank. And when I left Cairo, you were continuously on my mind. Your poem kept me alive and sane, I read it every day. My husband was working with his associates on important research. He told me that when finished it would save millions of people, especially in Africa. I told him I would stay with him until he finished his research, then we would divorce, and he agreed. You know Frank, I was a fool, I should have divorced him as soon as I came back from Cairo.

Carla took another sip of water, and was anxious to continue. 'A few months ago strange things started to happen which scared me, but they scared him more. He seemed to know what was happening and what he was afraid of, but he didn't want to worry me. Our house was searched many times by somebody, and everything was always put back neatly the way it was. Whoever searched our house probably thought we wouldn't know. But we knew. And whenever we went out somebody was following us. When I insisted that he tells me what was going on, he told me that people in high positions in the government were very interested in his medical research. My husband refused to cooperate with them because he didn't trust them; he didn't know for sure whether they were government agents or foreign agents. When the research was completed successfully, he told his two associates to leave San Diego. He was afraid something might happen to them. Here is the worst part. Three weeks ago, my husband died in a car accident. According to police, he was speeding on Highway 5 just south of Santa Ana. Police says he lost control, hit a truck, and rolled over many times before the car burst into flames. He was pulled out of the car but there was nothing left of him; he was completely incinerated.'

I interrupted Carla, 'Was your husband Dr Stephen Kramer?'

'Yes, he was,' Carla replied, 'did you know him?'

'No, I didn't know him, but I read about the accident in the paper, and it was on television. What a terrible accident that was.'

Carla looked at me and said, 'Frank, I don't believe it was an accident. Stephen was a careful driver, and he kept his car in good mechanical condition. And he would never go over the speed limit, never.'

'Are you absolutely sure it was not an accident?'

'Yes, I'm sure. Since Stephen died, I feel I'm still being watched and followed everywhere I go. I know they followed me here.'

Carla paused for few seconds then told me, 'Frank, I want to hire you to find out exactly what happened to Stephen. I have a feeling he didn't die in the car accident. I think he was murdered. I don't know how they did it, but I really believe he was murdered. Would you help me, Frank?'

'Of course I will, Carla. Now tell me about the last time you were with Stephen. Did you notice anything different about him, anything unusual?'

'I remember we were having breakfast that morning, it was about nine o'clock. He was very happy and excited because he finally finished the life-saving research he was working on. He was proud of himself and his associates because it was very successful. He was talking about both of us going on a vacation to Hawaii. I was about to remind him that I wanted the divorce when the telephone rang. After talking for about a minute, he told me that he had to go and meet someone at a restaurant by Highway 5, and that he would be back by 4 o'clock.'

'Do you know if an autopsy was done on him?'

'No. He was badly burned, and I think that someone, I don't know who, decided that an autopsy was not necessary. Maybe this person had something to do with his death, and didn't want an autopsy done.'

'Well, we can't prove that, Carla. But I will see what can be done.'

As I paced around the room, I was thinking about Carla's safety. She could be in danger staying alone in San Diego.

'Carla,' I said, 'I suggest you spend some time here. I am concerned about your safety, being alone in San Diego.'

'But I didn't bring any clothes with me.'

'Don't worry. Oliver will take care of that.'

'Who's Oliver?' Carla asked curiously.

'Oliver is our butler, our cook, our chauffeur, and our best investigator - he's all in one. You met him when you came in.'

I pushed a button on the desk and Oliver came in. I introduced them, and then told Oliver, 'Carla is a friend of mine. Would you please take her to Madame Truddie, and tell her to sort Carla out with all the clothes that she needs.'

Carla looked at me with those beautiful blue eyes, gave me a kiss, and left the room with Oliver.

I went outside and watched them leave in the limousine. I just stood there, still in shock, thinking about how the last two hours had affected me. I felt transformed; my heart pounded with joy - of course, my Carla was with me again.

I went back to the house whistling with happiness and dancing in circles. BJ was standing by the door, he saw Carla and Oliver leave. BJ was looking at me wondering what had gone wrong with me. He must have thought I was going nuts.

CHAPTER ELEVEN

I went to the pool area and asked Rachel and Jackie to join us in the living room. As we gathered I said, with joy in my voice, 'Well, we now have a new case, a big case.' Everybody smiled and looked happy.

'But first, I must tell you something. Our client is Carla. We met in Cairo about six years ago, when I was doing research for my university thesis. We fell in love, but unfortunately due to personal reasons we lost contact after she returned to America. Anyway, she's here now, and she needs our help. I asked Oliver to take her to town to buy some clothes from Mrs Truddie. She will be staying with us because it's dangerous for her to be alone in her house in San Diego.'

BJ interrupted, 'Wait a minute, Frank. Do you mean that the girl I saw walking out with Oliver is Carla, the one you were telling me about? Wow oh wow, she is a knockout.' Everybody laughed.

'Yes BJ, she's the one, and I have to agree, after six years she's still a knockout. Now, let's get to business. Do you remember a few weeks ago in the newspapers and on television a report about a Dr Stephen Kramer who died in a car accident on Highway 5 just south of Santa Ana?'

'You mean the man who was completely burned out in his car?' BJ asked.

'Yes, that's the one. Well, Dr Kramer was Carla's husband. Carla is convinced that he was murdered. So, our job is to prove that she is right.'

'But the news reported that he was speeding and lost control,' Jackie said.

'How could she be so sure?' Rachel asked.

'Well, Carla told me that for quite some time before his death, Dr Kramer and his two associates were working in medical research.

They were convinced that the research was so important that it would eventually save many lives, and would also make some people very rich. When they completed the research it was a total success. However, somebody knew they were working on this research and desperately wanted the results. Dr Kramer refused to cooperate with them and he advised his associates to leave San Diego for their own safety. Before Dr Kramer's death, Carla said that their house was searched many times, and that they were followed everywhere they went. I really believe Carla.'

'Does she have any information about who was behind this?' BJ asked.

'No, but Dr Kramer told her that these people were in the government, but did not go into details,' I answered.

'That research must be very important - valuable enough to kill for,' Jackie commented.

'I agree with you, Jackie. Carla told me that the last time she saw her husband was when he received a telephone call, and then left the house to meet someone in a restaurant along Highway 5.'

'So, how can we help her, and where do we start?' Rachel asked.

We were all quiet. I then suggested, 'Why don't we do this? On Monday, we all drive to San Diego, to Carla's house. Jackie, I want you and Rachel to install surveillance cameras in every room in Carla's house, and make sure they are well hidden. Set the monitors inside the van. These people, I suspect, have already put a bug on every phone, so if you find these bugs, don't remove them. We could use the bugs to our advantage, but be careful what you say while you're there.'

Everybody was quiet, so I said, 'Well, what do you think? This is an interesting case, but it could also be a dangerous one. These people will kill to get what they want. We have to be very careful, and watch out for each other. I need your input.'

'I was digesting what you said. This sounds like a good plan, but we have to see how it goes, step by step,' BJ said.

Jackie and Rachel agreed.

Carla and Oliver returned shortly after 5 o'clock. When I opened the door and saw Carla standing there, smiling and looking like a queen, my heart beat with joy. Oliver had his hands full of shopping bags. I told him to take the bags to the main guest room which was next to mine. Oliver looked at me as he walked past. I escorted Carla to the living room. 'Did you have a good time?' I asked.

'Oh yes, and especially Oliver. He made me laugh all the time we were out.'

'That's good. You can't hide that beautiful smile, and those beautiful blue eyes.'

I sat beside Carla on the couch, held her hands and said, 'I'm so happy you are here, and now that I've found you again, I am not going to let you out of my sight.' And as I gently touched her lips with my fingers, Carla said, 'I love you Frank, with all my heart.' And then we kissed.

We heard footsteps. BJ, Jackie, Rachel and Oliver were coming in. I introduced BJ, Jackie, and Rachel to Carla, and then I suggested, 'How about if we all go to Luigi's restaurant for dinner? Luigi has the best Italian food in town.'

'That's a very good idea,' BJ said, 'I'll call and make a reservation.'

'Please excuse me. I need to freshen up and change before we go,' Carla said.

After Carla left, BJ looked at me and said, 'Where on earth did you find such a beauty? She is gorgeous. Maybe I should go to Cairo for a visit.'

'It has been a long time, but I still love her very much. After all these years, she hasn't changed a bit; in fact, she's even more beautiful now,' I commented.

At the restaurant I told Luigi to serve us his best meal together with the best wine. Luigi looked at me and said, 'I will make you the best dinner ever. You won't forget it.' Luigi kept his word. He served us a most wonderful dinner: chicken cordon bleu on a special home-made pasta covered with a delicate cheese sauce, and surrounded by large marinated shrimps. A mixed salad was also served, smothered with Luigi's own salad dressing. It was an absolutely delicious meal. There was so much to savour, we had to eat it slowly. No room for dessert. A very expensive white wine was also served and consumed.

BJ commented, 'Where does Luigi get this wine from? I really need to know.'

I answered BJ, 'He won't tell you, BJ, but he will sell it to you, for about $200 a bottle.'

'Well, that's cheap. I'll just charge it to business expenses, not a big deal,' BJ said jokingly.

Carla was at the centre of attention; everybody in the restaurant was staring at her. Her beauty seemed to stand out wherever we went.

When we returned to the house, Carla was feeling tired, so she went straight to her bedroom. I also went to my bedroom, had a shower and fixed myself a drink of Chivas Regal, and I fixed one for Carla - I knew she would come. A few minutes later there was a light knock on my door. I opened it and saw Carla, dressed in a pink silk summer nightdress.

'I couldn't sleep Frank, and I feel lonely. Can I come in?'

'What took you so long?' I said, while carrying her to the couch, and bringing her the drink.

She had a sip while looking at me. I couldn't resist her beautiful blue eyes and those desirable lips. I put the drinks on the table and we hugged and kissed.

We kissed passionately and we made love. It brought back wonderful memories, as if we were in Cairo, and as if we were making love for the first time.

The next day, Sunday, was just another beautiful sunny day in Beverly Hills. Carla and I slept late, and we didn't come down until the early afternoon. We spent the afternoon by the pool. Oliver was at the barbecue: jumbo shrimp, tender lamb chops, filet mignon, and chicken, all marinated. He also produced baked potatoes, corn on the cub and asparagus. And he had made his own salad.

Carla said, jokingly, 'Oliver is a super chef and he is a jack of all trades. Watch out Luigi, Oliver is coming.'

Jackie commented, 'Don't forget his sense of humour too. We all love him.'

Oliver put all the food on a large table, then he rang a bell, and said, 'Sunday brunch is ready, come and get it.' We all had a little of everything that Oliver had cooked. Everything was just delicious.

BJ commented, 'Are we eating at Luigi's? This is wonderful,' and he laughed and said, 'Oliver, how about us boys play snooker with the girls. Do you think we can beat them?'

'Oh, I don't know about that. I bet you $5 that we can beat you, best 2 out of 3. Are you ready for the challenge?' BJ said.

'We're ready, let's go,' Rachel said with confidence.

We saw the four of them go to the sports room.

Carla and I had a beautiful relaxed afternoon. We went to my room when it was starting to get dark. We undressed and laid in bed totally naked, hugging each other, kissing and making love.

CHAPTER TWELVE

It was about noon on Monday, and we were getting ready to drive to Carla's house in San Diego. Jackie and Rachel loaded the van with their equipment and were ready to move out. Oliver, BJ, Carla and I went in one of the Lexus SUVs. Oliver was driving.

In the SUV, BJ sat in the front while Carla and I sat in the back. Carla sat close to me, holding onto my hand, and resting her head on my shoulder.

'You look beautiful Carla,' I whispered in her ear.

'You look beautiful too darling,' and she kissed me.

I knew she felt happy and safe, now that she was with me. After a while she said, 'Frank, when this is all over, let's take a vacation and go to Cairo. I really miss it.'

'Of course we will go to Cairo, and we will take a Felucca ride, and you can belly dance. But there's one thing I'm worried about.'

'And what's that?' Carla asked.

'Well, if you become a good dancer like Samia, the Egyptians might pay you a lot of money in order to keep you in Cairo.'

'There's not enough money in the world that would keep me away from you, Frank,' Carla said, and then rested her head on my shoulder again while I put my arm around her waist.

As we unloaded the luggage and equipment, BJ looked at me and said, 'Did you notice? We were being followed from the time we left Beverly Hills.'

'Yes, I did notice. Whoever they are, better let them think we didn't know they were following us.'

Inside the house, I said to Jackie and Rachel, in a low voice, 'Just to let you know, we were followed since we left Beverly Hills, so be careful. BJ and I are going to visit Captain Jim Shannon.'

We were about to leave when Carla came to me and kissed me. I told her we wouldn't be long. As we drove away, Oliver said, 'Frank, that same car just pulled out behind us.'

'That's alright, Oliver, just drive normally.'

We entered the San Diego Police Department and I told the desk sergeant that Captain Shannon was expecting us. Captain Shannon had been in the police force for over 25 years and we became friends during the kidnapping case. Sadly, his wife passed away recently. He is a dedicated and honest police officer. He always spoke of his work as his second wife.

Captain Shannon looked pleased to see us. He stood up as we entered his office, shook our hands, and said, 'It is nice to see both of you again. Another kidnapping case?'

'No, not this time, Jim. This time it's more complicated and we need your help,' I said as we sat down.

'First, how about coffee?' Jim asked.

'I'll have mine black,' BJ said.

'Me too,' I said, and continued while Jim was pouring the coffee. 'We have been hired by Mrs Kramer, you know, the wife of Dr Kramer, the one who was burned to death in a car accident on Highway 5 near Santa Ana.'

'Oh yes, I remember that. It was an awful accident. Poor guy,' Jim said while handing us the coffee.

'Jim, Mrs Kramer thinks that it was not an accident. She believes her husband was murdered.'

'Murdered?' Jim said curiously as he looked at me.

'Yes, murdered,' I told him. 'It was made to look like an accident. You see Jim, many things happened before and after the death of her husband which have made her suspect he was murdered.'

I went into detail with Jim about the things that had happened, especially the search of her house.

'We didn't authorise any search of her house. Does she know who was doing that?' Jim asked.

'No, Jim. She doesn't know who they were.'

'Well, see if you can find out, and let me know. Things like car registration number, photos, any small things, OK?'

'I'll do that, Jim. And one more thing. Mrs Kramer would like an autopsy done on her husband as soon as possible.'

'I'll get on it right away. I know a local judge very well. I'll get him to approve the autopsy and will call you as soon as it is completed.'

Before we left, I stressed to Jim, 'Please don't discuss this with anyone. We don't know what or who we are dealing with. Dr Kramer told his wife that people in the our government were involved.'

'Don't worry, Frank. You can depend on me.'

While heading back to Carla's house, Oliver said we were being followed again. I asked Oliver to pull to the side and stop. After we stopped, Oliver opened the trunk of the limousine, and I got out pretending to get something from the trunk. The car following us, a blue Ford Mustang, passed us. I had a good look at the two men inside, and the licence plate.

It was about 4 o'clock when we returned to Carla's house. The girls were in the living room each having a glass of wine, and three glasses were waiting for us. We were drinking wine when Jackie said, 'Let's go out to the pool area,' while pointing at the telephones. Outside she started to tell us what she and Rachel did. She had a remote in her hand. 'A push on this remote will activate a camera in each room,' Jackie said while handing me the remote. 'We put the monitors in the van and we can view every room and hear everything that is said. And everything will be recorded on tape.'

'What about bugs in the telephones, did you find any?' I asked.

'We found a bug in every phone,' Rachel answered, 'and we left them there.'

'That's good, let them think we don't know what they are doing. Just be careful what you say. You girls did a good job. Now let's park the van in the garage, lock it, activate the cameras, and then we can all go out to dinner.'

An hour later we activated the cameras, and drove off to dinner. As we drove, we noticed the blue Mustang parked at the end of the block. We pretended we didn't see them. We had dinner at Carla's favourite Chinese restaurant. It was super; we enjoyed it very much.

It must have been after 8 o'clock when we returned to the house. As we got out of the vehicle, I told Jackie and Rachel, 'Once inside the house, check and see if they have moved anything or left anything.'

After checking all the rooms, Jackie reported that the bugs in every room and in the phones were still there. We then went to the van in the garage to check the cameras and see who had visited while we out at dinner.

'Bingo, come and see,' Jackie said anxiously. We gathered around the screen and saw two men enter the house. I commented, 'Those are the two men that I saw in the Mustang that was following us.'

The two men appeared to search every room. They were wearing white gloves. After ten minutes they decided to leave. One of them made a phone call, and we heard him say, 'It's not here, so we're going to leave before they come back.' Then the two men left.

I put my finger under my chin, thinking, and then said to everybody, 'I'm curious to find out what they were looking for. Whatever it is, it has to be somewhere in this house. So, let's start with the study.'

The study was quite large. On one side of the room there was a desk, and behind it there were shelves full of books. In front of the desk there were two leather chairs. On the opposite side of the desk there was a long table flush with the wall, and another table, the same size, a few feet in front of it. There was medical equipment on the tables that I assume were used for tests and analysis. Dr Kramer and his two associates probably did a lot of their research in the study. We searched just about everywhere, but we couldn't find a thing.

'There has to be something here, Carla,' I said. 'Your husband was an intelligent man. Can you think of anything, no matter how small, that might give us a clue?'

I watched Carla's face. As she appeared to be thinking about something, she stood up and walked slowly around the room, and then stopped by one of the bookcases and stared at the books. She pulled out a book.

'What is it Carla?' I asked her.

'Just a hunch. This is a book of love poems. I always read it whenever I am sad. Stephen knew that, so I thought he might have left something in it.'

Carla handed me the book. I slowly the turned the pages. In the last page of the book there was a small piece of paper folded over and taped up. I pulled it out and handed it to Carla.

Carla opened the paper and showed it to me, careful not to say anything out loud in case she was being overheard by the bugs. 'Dear Carla, pull out the bottom left hand drawer of the desk, turn it over, and you will find a letter. Please be very careful. Read the letter and then burn it. Love, Stephen.'

BJ went to desk, pulled out the bottom left hand drawer and turned it upside down. Sure enough, there was an envelope. BJ opened the envelope, and found a letter inside. He gave it to Carla.

'Go ahead and read it,' I told Carla.

We were all anxious to know what was in the letter. We walked out to the pool area and gathered around Carla. 'It's safe, they cannot hear us here,' I stated. Carla started to read.

'My darling Carla. First I would like to apologise for not spending enough time with you. I devoted all my time to my research and neglected you. I knew you were upset with me, but I also know you are patient and understanding. Thank you for putting up with me all these years.

'I am writing you this letter because I have a feeling that sooner or later something will happen to me. I might even be killed. As I told you, my associates, Jack, Hank, and I were working on medical research, a very important study that would rid the world of a deadly disease. However, a group of wealthy and powerful people, who I suspected work for the government, knew what we were doing. They spied on us 24 hours a day.

'To complete our research, we wanted to conduct a test on a young black man in Kisangani, Zaire. His name is Madoda

Kasongo. He was infected with this disease and was about to die. He gave us written permission to do the treatment. The Zaire Ministry of Health also gave us permission to treat him. We agreed that if the treatment was successful, we would ask the US government to check it out and get FDA approval, and maybe save millions of people. We secretly kept Madoda in hospital in Zaire where we conducted our treatment. Zaire security guarded Madoda's room round the clock. We gave Madoda an injection of the vaccine every day for 30 days. We tested him every day, and we noticed that every day the virus was fading away. At the end of 30 days we stopped giving the injections because the virus had completely disappeared from his system. We didn't want to rush and tell the world about our discovery; we wanted to wait for at least a week to see if his improved condition was sustained. After a week there were no changes, and that meant our treatment was a total success. Madoda started to live normally with no further treatment necessary.

'However, soon after Madoda was cured, he disappeared. Nobody knew where he went. I have a feeling he was kidnapped by the group that was following us. But how? He was well guarded 24 hours a day. Probably the guards were paid off. With this letter you will find a picture of Madoda, and the key to our safety deposit box at our bank. In the box you will find the only copy of the video tape of our whole discovery from day one. It contains all the details of the research, the treatment we gave Madoda, and his ultimate recovery. There are no other copies made. I suggest you make a copy of this video. And please take care of it. The lives of millions depend on it.

'The wealthy people I was telling you about want the tape desperately. They will kill for it, and they don't care who they kill.

'When I started getting threatening telephone calls, I told Jack and Hank to leave San Diego; I didn't want to see them get hurt. You have their telephone numbers. Take the video tape from the safety deposit box and give it to the right person, to someone you trust. Again, I must stress - please be very careful. One more thing, look after Jennifer and give her my love. Love you, Stephen.'

Carla was in tears when she finished reading the letter, and in a loud voice she shouted, 'If he knew he was in danger, why didn't he go to the police or the FBI?'

Jackie and Rachel walked over to Carla to console her.

'Maybe he didn't know who to trust,' BJ commented.

'BJ is right, Carla,' I said. 'He did say in the letter that he suspected these people were in the government, and dangerous.'

Carla was still furious and crying as she said, 'But why didn't he go to the FBI? He just let himself be killed by these vicious people without telling anybody. He should have done something.'

'Don't you worry Carla, we will find these people.' BJ said.

'Carla, we can't change what has happened, and we can't let Stephen's work go to waste,' I said. 'He worked hard to complete his research, and he succeeded. Now, we'll make him famous for what he did.'

There was silence. We all felt the pain Carla was going through. I whispered to Jackie and Rachel to escort Carla to her bedroom, and to stay with her until she felt better. I didn't want Carla to be alone.

The next day, around noon, Jackie and Rachel drove the van around the block and parked in a secluded area. Carla, BJ, Oliver and I left the house in the SUV. We knew we were being watched because the same Mustang was parked up the street. They saw us leave, but they did not follow us. We pulled up behind the van. Jackie had all the monitors working, and we could see every room in the house.

'Now we sit and wait,' I said, 'I hope you have plenty of coffee and sandwiches, Oliver.'

'Yes, of course,' Oliver answered.

An hour passed and we were still waiting. Shortly afterwards, BJ said, 'Guys, bingo, they're going into the house.'

We all looked at the monitors. This time, there were three men. One of them appeared to give orders because we heard him say, 'Check everywhere, don't miss a spot.' Thirty minutes later, the man in charge called off the search and told the other two men to go back to headquarters.

It looked like they did not find what they were looking for.

Fifteen minutes after they left, we returned to the house. The Mustang was not in sight. As soon as we came in, I told Rachel and Jackie to develop two photos of each of the three men.

'What do you think, BJ?' I asked.

'I think we should have come back here and broken their bones.'

'Not yet, BJ. We don't want these guys to know we were watching them. We want them guys to take us to their leader. So first thing in the morning I'll go and see Jim Shannon. Maybe he can help us. Now, how about pizza for everyone?'

'That's an excellent idea,' Oliver agreed. 'This way I don't have to cook. I'll order the pizza.'

After everybody left the room, I sat by Carla. Her face was downcast, and she appeared sad and confused.

'Blue Eyes, we are going to find out who is behind this.' I gently touched her chin and moved her up to face me. 'Don't look sad. You are with me now and I will never let anything happen to you. I love you with all my heart.'

Looking at me with tears in her eyes, Carla said, 'I know, Frank, and I love you very much.' We hugged and kissed.

There was something in Dr Kramer's letter that was bothering me, so I asked Carla, 'In the letter from Stephen, what did he mean when he said, "Look after Jennifer and give her my love". Who is this Jennifer?'

'A six-year old girl we were planning to adopt,' Carla answered.

We were interrupted when Rachel and Jackie brought the photos of the three men. They also brought two bottles of wine and six glasses.

'That was quick,' I said. 'The photos look very clear. I'll show them to Jim tomorrow.' We were about to have a glass of wine when Oliver came in with the pizza.

I woke up early the next morning, and so as not to disturb the others, I quietly left the house. On my way to the San Diego Police Department I picked up two dozen donuts.

Jim was not in yet, but the sergeant escorted me to Jim's office. I handed the sergeant a dozen donuts, 'That's for you and the guys.' He liked that and thanked me. As the sergeant was pouring me a cup of coffee, Jim walked in. He looked at me with a smile and said, 'Well, you're here early.'

'Someone has to look after you, my friend. I bet you didn't have breakfast.'

'You're right. I had a glass of orange juice. That was enough for me,' Jim said.

'You seem to neglect yourself since Martha left. Look at you, you are shrinking. Here, have a donut and coffee.'

The sergeant, with a grin in his face, handed Jim a cup of coffee, looked at me, and walked out.

'Maybe you should come and visit me every morning,' Jim smiled.

'I have to tell you something very important Jim, and I need your help. Whatever I tell you, it's between you and me only. Are you with me, Jim?'

'You sound like you have an exciting story to tell me. You don't have to worry about me, Frank, you can trust me. If I can help you, I'll do my best. What's on your mind?'

I opened the brown envelope that I was carrying. I brought out the photos of the three men and handed them to Jim, and said, 'Do you recognise any of these men?'

After looking at the photos carefully, Jim looked at me and said, while pointing at one of the men in a photo, 'I recognise this one, he's an FBI agent, assigned here in San Diego. I don't know the other two. Where did you get these photos?'

'These three men searched Carla Kramer's house yesterday, illegally, while she was out. They didn't know that we had cameras hidden around the house.' I paused. 'Now, why would the FBI search her house illegally? I need your help, Jim, and I need to find answers to these questions quickly. I believe Carla Kramer is in grave danger. I also believe that her husband was murdered.'

'Do you have an idea what they were looking for?'

'Yes, I do, but I'd better not tell you now because if I tell you, you could be in danger. Do you know anyone in the FBI in San Diego, someone you can trust? This case may involve people higher up in the FBI, so you have to be careful.'

I know Bill Sawyer, he is the FBI Chief of the San Diego branch. We went to school together; we're like brothers. He is a straight man and we can trust him. Do you want me to find out who these two men in the photos are, and who they work for?'

'Yes, Jim, try to find out but in a way so as not to raise suspicion. You never know who is listening and watching.'

As I was leaving, I turned to Jim and asked him if he had the results of the autopsy.

'No, not yet. I'll call you as soon as I get the report. But since they are listening, I will talk about another subject, and you'll get my message.'

CHAPTER THIRTEEN

Later that afternoon, I received a telephone call from Jim.

'Hi Frank, how would and your team like to come over tonight for dinner? I do a good BBQ, say around 7?'

'That would be great, we need a break. See you at 7.'

I gathered my team by the pool area. 'I guess it's safe to talk here. Jim just called me and invited us for a BBQ at his house. He has some news for us. Bill Sawyer, Chief of San Diego FBI branch will also be there. Jim didn't want to discuss it over the telephone, you know, they may be listening. So, let's be ready to go around 6:30.'

An hour later, as I walked by the kitchen, I saw Carla cooking something. I approached her and asked, 'What are doing?'

'Oh, I just thought of making a lasagne and apple pie to take with us.'

'That is kind of you. Have you finished?'

'Yes,' Carla answered. 'So now, come with me because I want to show you something.'

We went upstairs and she took me to the bedroom. 'You just sit here for a minute.' Carla said, and disappeared.

So I sat down. A few minutes later she came back, dressed in a short sexy small top and knickers in a sizzling sparkling red material.

'Do you like it?' she asked me.

'I love it, and I love you. Are you going to belly dance for me?'

She walked back about five feet, and started to belly dance, using all the sexy moves she learned in Cairo. She looked desirable, and I just couldn't resist anymore. I walked to her, put my hands around her waist, and we kissed so passionately. We laid on the bed as I undressed, and we made love for a long time, until we fell asleep. Around 4 o'clock we woke up. Carla was laying on top of me, naked; she wanted to stay in bed longer, but I suggested we had to get ready. We both got up and had a shower.

Jim didn't live far away, about 20 minutes' drive. So around 6:30 we were all ready to drive to his place. We took the SUV, but Carla forgot to take the lasagne and pie, so we went back to the house and picked up the food.

Just before 7 o'clock we arrived at Jim's house. Jim welcomed us at the door and escorted us to the living room where he introduced us to Bill Sawyer. Jim showed us where the bar was, and said, 'There is plenty of Chivas Regal, beer, and whatever else you desire, so help yourself.'

As we sat down, Jim said, 'The results of the autopsy showed that Dr Kramer died before the accident. He was poisoned. He had enough poison in his system to kill him in few minutes. We have no proof how he was poisoned, but from what I can determine, Dr Kramer went to meet a person at the restaurant, and when Dr Kramer refused to give him what he wanted, I assume the person probably put the poison in his drink, or he had someone to do it, maybe a waiter. And while Dr Kramer was driving on Highway 5, the poison took its effect, resulting in the accident and his death.'

I asked Jim, 'But why would they kill Dr Kramer if he has what they desperately needed? That doesn't make sense.'

'Well, Frank, Dr Kramer must have told them he would never give it to them. So they decided to get rid of him before he told the authorities about them. Also, they probably assumed that Dr Kramer must have hidden the information in a safe place, like a bank deposit box. It would be easy for them to get it from the person who takes it from the deposit box. These people are professionals, they know what they are doing.'

Everyone was silent in the room, and we looked at each other in disbelief. Bill Sawyer broke the silence pointing to one of the men in the pictures we had taken. 'This man is an FBI agent. He works for me, and I will find out what he is doing, without raising any suspicion. But I don't know the other two men.'

'Do you think they are FBI agents too?' Jim asked.

'If I have to make a guess, I would say they are FBI agents, but from which area?' I commented.

After a short pause, I decided it was time to tell Jim and Bill all that we knew.

'Jim, Bill, there's something I have to tell you now. Sorry I didn't tell you this before, but I didn't realise the extent of the problem, and was worried about your safety. We are facing professional killers.'

I paused for few seconds, and then continued, 'Please, keep a secret what I am about to tell you until we get to the bottom of this.'

'Well, Frank, we'll keep the secret. What's on your mind?' Jim asked.

'Carla told me that Dr Kramer and his two associates were working on some sort of important medical research. They travelled all over the world, and they finally ended up in Zaire, where they successfully completed their research and came up with a vaccine to cure a deadly virus. They assembled the complete research, the data and the vaccine formula into a video tape. However, three things happened since they completed the research. First, a young African man from Zaire called Madoda caught this virus, and was dying of it. Dr Kramer injected Madoda with a vaccine for 30 days, and he was totally cured. But shortly afterwards, Madoda disappeared. Second, Dr Kramer's house was searched many times, probably looking for the video tape. And third, Dr Kramer was murdered.'

Whoever these people are, they want that video very badly. Since they couldn't get it from Dr Kramer, they assume that Mrs Kramer will eventually take it from the bank, and they will take it from her. That's why she is in danger now.'

'Well, I was right,' Jim said, 'Dr Kramer refused to give them the video tape, so they killed him. And by the way Frank, do you have a picture of Madoda?'

I opened an envelope and showed them the photo of Madoda.

'Where is this video tape now?' Bill asked.

'It's locked in a safety deposit box in a bank here in San Diego. Carla is the only one that can get it out. I suggest we leave it there until we find out who is behind all this.'

'And how do we start to find out who their leader is?' BJ asked.

After a minute of silence, Jim said, 'Why don't we lure these three men into Carla's house and then arrest them. They don't have a search warrant, so we would have a reason to keep them in jail until someone bails them out.'

'That's a good idea, Jim,' Bill said.

'Can we break their bones before you arrest them? Call it resisting arrest,' BJ said jokingly, and everybody laughed.

'Well, let's not waste time,' I said. 'How about tomorrow afternoon. We'll make them think that Carla has the video tape, lure them into the house, and give them some time to search the house, and then we'll arrest them. Can you have your men close by, and I'll give you a call as soon as they are in the house?'

'That would be great. We'll be there,' Jim answered.

We agreed on the plan to trap the three men.

The next morning we set the trap in motion. The Mustang was parked down the road with the three men inside. Around 11 o'clock, Carla and I drove off in Carla's car and headed towards the bank. The Mustang followed us, as we expected. We parked near the bank and went inside. Carla carried a blank video tape inside her bag.

While in the bank, I looked out of the window and saw the Mustang parked across the street. We needed to spend some time inside the bank, so Carla went to see the bank manager and chatted with him. He knew her and Dr Kramer very well, as he had attended many of their parties.

About 15 minutes later, Carla and I came out of the bank. Carla was carrying the blank video tape. It was not inside her bag; she made sure it was visible to the men in the Mustang. To make even more sure they saw the video tape, she dropped it on the ground on purpose, then she picked it up again.

We drove back to the house. The Mustang followed us. When we arrived, Oliver had lunch ready, so we all sat by the pool and enjoyed the lunch.

An hour later we all came out of the house. Oliver, BJ, Carla and I went in the SUV, while Rachel and Jackie took the van. We drove few blocks away from the house and parked in a secluded area. Inside the van, we all waited, confident that the three men would move to search Carla's house.

Jim and his men were hiding near the house. I asked Jim if he and his men were ready. Jim assured me that they were ready, and would wait for my signal.

Shortly after we talked, we saw the three men enter the house and start their search for the video tape. I called Jim and told him that the three men were inside the house.

In less than a minute, Jim and seven of his officers rushed into the house with their guns pointed at the three men. The men did not resist; they just raised their hands up.

'What are you doing in this house? Do you have a search warrant?' Jim asked them.

They showed Jim their FBI badges, and their leader complained to Jim, 'We are FBI agents on official business, and you have no right to interfere.'

'I have every right, mister. You're all under arrest.'

Jim then directed his officers to read the

three men their rights, handcuff them, and take them to the station.

After the officers drove off with the three FBI agents, we returned to the house. Jim smiled and said as he was about to leave, 'Well, it went as planned, now the fun begins. I'll keep you informed.'

We gathered in the living room. I told Jackie and Rachel not to remove the bugs in the phones or the cameras, saying, 'You don't know what might happen. We'll take them when all is clear.'

Oliver decided to cook one of his famous meals. He told us it was a secret. As we walked to the swimming pool, I told Oliver, 'Call us when you're ready.'

CHAPTER FOURTEEN

The next morning Bill Sawyer went to see his FBI agent in jail, pretending he knew nothing about what happened the day before.

'Mike, why are you in jail?'

Mike was very nervous and worried as he looked at his boss, and said, 'Chief, can we talk privately?'

'Sure, let's go to an empty room.'

Mike started to explain to his boss, 'It all started with my cousin. He is one of the other two FBI agents that were arrested. My FBI cousin is assigned to Washington DC. About three months ago he told me that a big operation was going on in San Diego, and they needed the help of a local FBI agent. He said it was a top secret operation handled directly from FBI Headquarters by the FBI Director himself. He also told me that the FBI Chief in San Diego, that's you, knew all about this operation, but nobody was allowed to discuss it with anybody. That's why I never talked to you about it. But in any case he never told me exactly the details of what the operation was all about. He just said he wanted me to find the other agents a hotel, take them around, and help them with anything they needed, but never to get the local FBI branch involved.'

Bill handed Mike a cigarette. As he smoked, Mike said, 'My cousin insisted that I tell no one because if the word leaked out, people might get killed. Chief, I honestly thought you knew about it, so I kept quiet and did what he told me. You have to believe me, Chief.'

'Did they tell you what kind of operation they were working on, or who was in charge?' Bill asked.

'No, but I remember he told me that it had the interest of people higher up in the FBI, and someone in the White House. He also told me that I should not ask any more questions. I swear to you, that's all I remember.'

Bill looked at Mike, who was shaking, put his hand on his shoulder and said, 'I believe what you told me Mike. But, listen to me, there is something fishy and illegal going on. No, I did not know about the operation; your cousin lied to you. They went behind my back to recruit you; you were an easy catch, being a cousin. If this thing they are secretly working on turns out to be against the law, you could be in a lot of trouble.'

'Yes, Chief. I'm sorry to have caused you these problems.'

'Listen Mike. I'm going to talk to Jim Shannon, the San Diego Police Chief, and ask him to let you out, but not right away.

Don't worry, you won't be charged with anything, but here's what I want you to do. From now on, remember, you are working for me, and not the DC FBI. I want you to stay in jail until someone releases the three of you. Pretend you still work for them, and don't tell them you talked to me, OK? Try to find out as much information as you can, and who is in charge of this operation.'

'OK, Chief, I'll do that.' Mike said it in a sincere voice, and added, 'You believe me, don't you?'

'Yes Mike, I do believe you, I already told you that. But in the future, don't keep anything from me, no matter how small it is, or who told you, understand?'

'I understand,' Mike replied.

After the guard took Mike back to his cell, Bill went to see Jim. He told Jim about the conversation he had with Mike.

'Mike is a good rookie. He honestly thought he was doing his job. I believe him.

Keep him in jail until all three are released. Maybe he can dig out some information from them.'

While they were talking, the telephone rang and Jim answered it. The caller was Tom Collins, the FBI Director in Washington, DC. Jim looked surprised. He put the speakerphone on, and looked at Bill.

The voice came on. 'Hello Jim, this is Tom Collins from DC. How are you?'

'I'm just fine Tom,' Jim said, 'What a surprise. I don't get a chance to talk to the FBI Director very often. So what can I do for you?'

'Jim, I was just told that you have some of my agents in your jail.'

Jim said in a surprised voice, 'I didn't know they worked for you, Tom. We arrested these men after they broke into a house. We received a call that there was a break in, so we went to investigate. They did not have a search warrant, and the identification cards they showed us could have been fake, so we had no choice but to arrest them, and keep them in custody until we checked them out.'

I understand, Jim. You were doing your job, but believe me, we are doing our job too. We are working on a classified operation that involves national security. It is so secret that only a few people know about it. Why don't I vouch for these agents, and I'd appreciate it if you released them as soon as possible.'

'Well, OK Tom, I'll let them go. By the way, can we help you in any way with this secret operation?'

'No, we can handle it. Thanks again, Jim. Listen, if you ever visit DC, stop by headquarters. I'd love to see you.'

'Funny you mention that Tom. Two British friends of mine just arrived from England. They asked if we could take them to tour the capital next week. We'll stop by and pay you a visit. They will be thrilled to visit FBI Headquarters.'

'I look forward to seeing you and your British friends next week. Goodbye.'

Jim turned the speakerphone off, looked at Bill, and smiled as he asked, 'Do you think we are getting closer to the leaders?'

Bill was curious as he said, 'I didn't know you were going to take a vacation next week. And yes, we seem to be getting closer. Could you explain?'

'I wasn't going on vacation, but I am now.' Jim answered excitedly, smiling, and rubbing his hands together. He added, 'This is getting to be very interesting Bill. Just think about it, why would the FBI Director himself call me and ask about his agents. His deputy or secretary could have done that. He must have something to hide.'

'Jim, do you think he's the only one that knows about this operation? Maybe when you visit him next week, he might tell you something about this "National Security" operation they are working on.'

'I don't think he is the only one that knows about it. I do hope he tells me, but I doubt it. I am going to call Frank and BJ and tell them that they are going with me to Washington DC next week.'

Jim lifted the telephone and called Frank.

'Frank, this is Jim. You won't believe who just called me. The FBI Director himself, Tom Collins. He asked me to release the three agents. He said they were working on a secret operation, but he did not explain what kind of operation.'

I was having lunch when Jim called me. I almost choked when I heard what he told me. I commented, 'How about that. Do you think he's involved?'

'Of course he's involved. What we need to do now is find out how much is he involved.'

After a short pause, Jim said, 'I have an idea Frank. How would you and BJ like to go with me to Washington DC next week on a vacation?'

'What's the occasion?' I asked Jim.

'Well, Tom invited me to visit him whenever I am in the DC area. I thought this would be a good opportunity to find out more about the case. So I told him two of my British friends are visiting me, and they want to tour the Capital and FBI Headquarters. He didn't expect to see me so quickly, but we'll go and see what we can find out.'

'That's a good idea. I'll also get tickets for Carla, Oliver, Jackie and Rachel to come with us. And by the way, did you find out anything more from the three FBI agents in jail?'

No, not yet. I am going to keep them in jail for few more hours, then I'll release them.

'Jim, Carla is going to call Dr Kramer's associates, hoping they might give us some information.'

'Good, Frank, let me know what she finds out.'

About two hours later Jim released the three FBI agents from jail. An hour later, as he was about to leave his office, Jim received a telephone call from Bill.

'Hi Jim, listen, my agent, Mike, just told me he overheard the two FBI agents talking about a group called the 'RST Group' and about a hospital just outside DC. He couldn't get the rest of it.'

'It looks like there is more to this. I hope we find out more when we visit DC.'

The next morning, Jim came to join us. We gathered in the living room while Carla telephoned Hank Milkowski, one of Dr Kramer's associates. He lived in Flagstaff, Arizona. Someone answered the telephone.

Carla introduced herself and asked to speak to Hank. After a minute, Carla said she was sorry, and hung up. She turned and looked at us and in a sad voice, she said, 'Hank's dead. His wife said that while on a hiking trip, Hank slipped and fell off a cliff, hit his head on a rock and died instantly.'

'Do you believe that?' BJ asked.

'No, I don't,' I answered, 'I think that whoever killed Dr Kramer must have killed Hank. He probably refused to tell them where the video tape was. What do you think Jim?'

'I agree with you Frank,' Jim said, and I believe his other associate, Jack, is in danger. Maybe we should call Jack.'

'Carla, go ahead and call Jack, and warn him.'

Carla was scared about calling Jack, because she was afraid something might have happened to him too, but she dialled

Jack's number, introduced herself and asked to speak to Jack. Again after a minute we heard Carla apologise and hang up.

Carla slowly sat down and started to cry. She said, 'It's too late; Jack's also dead. His mother said that a car hit him as he crossed a street in San Francisco. It was a hit and run, and the police could not find the car that hit him.'

I put my arms around Carla, trying to console her.

'Well, it looks like these people mean business; they will kill anybody that gets in their way.' Jackie commented.

'And we have to be extra careful,' BJ said.

'These two murders elevate this case to a higher dimension. We have to stop them,' Jim insisted. He then called Bill and told him about the two murders we had just found out about.

CHAPTER FIFTEEN

Carla had a difficult time sleeping. I tried to make her feel better, but I couldn't help. I told Carla that when we got to DC she was to stay with Oliver, Jackie and Rachel all the time. I then kissed her passionately and we made love.

The next morning we were all packed ready to go to the airport. Jim joined us, and we all went together in a rented limousine.

We had a wonderful flight, and each of us had a room in a luxury hotel not far from the White House. Carla and I had our own suite. We agreed to meet at the hotel restaurant for dinner around 7 o'clock.

As soon as we settled in, Jim called FBI headquarters and talked to Tom Collins. He made an appointment to meet with Tom the following morning at 11 o'clock.

Jim told us about the appointment with Tom as we had dinner. He suggested that Oliver, Jackie, Rachel and Carla take a tour of DC and meet us back at the hotel around 4 or 5 o'clock.

The following morning we had breakfast and then went to the lobby. The car that Jim rented was waiting for us. Jim was the driver; he knew his way around DC and drove us to FBI Headquarters.

Tom Collins rose from his chair as we entered his office. He shook Jim's hand, smiling and saying, 'Hello Jim, it is so nice to see you. It's been a long time.'

'Yes Tom, it has,' Jim agreed.

Jim introduced us to Tom, 'This is Frank and BJ. They're my friends from England, the ones I told you about.'

'Oh, yes, I remember. I visited England few years ago. I hope you enjoy your vacation in Washington,' Tom said.

'I'm sure we will. Jim knows the capital very well, and he plans to show us everything,' I said to Tom.

'By the way Tom, Frank and BJ are private investigators in England. Mrs Kramer has hired them to help with the murder of her husband, Dr Kramer.'

Tom looked surprised. His smile faded, and he said, 'I thought Dr Kramer's death was an accident, and the case was closed.'

'Well, we thought the same thing, Tom, but fresh evidence came up which forced us to reopen the case. Now, what about your two FBI agents, what were they doing in Mrs Kramer's house?'

Tom asked us if we wanted coffee, but we declined.

Tom rested back on his chair and said, 'For a long time we wondered why Dr Kramer and his two associates took so many trips overseas, especially to some weird places.

We thought they could have been doing something illegal, or maybe they were spies. Mind you, they were famous scientists. You know, it's one of those situations where the FBI becomes suspicious. After Dr Kramer's death, I wanted to close the case, but before doing that, we wanted to make sure they did not pass any classified information of valuable nature to foreign countries. So, we kept an eye on them. After his death, we thought his wife might have been involved. We sent the two agents to San Diego to check around. So far we found nothing. We plan to close the case and file it away.'

As Tom was talking, I stood and slowly walked around the room. A photograph on the fireplace mantel caught my eyes. It was a picture of Tom and two other men whom I recognised. One was Steve Martin, White House Chief of Staff, and the other was Dr Ramsey Jones, Secretary of Health, and a respected member of the black community. The three of them were fishing when the picture was taken.

When Tom finished talking, Jim said to him, 'I wish you would have asked us for help Tom. We could have done the search legally and helped you out.'

'No need for that now,' Tom commented. 'Like I said, we plan to close the case. But if we ever need your help again, I'll make sure we contact you.'

'Oh, by the way, I forgot to tell you. Dr Kramer's two associates also recently died under suspicious circumstances,' Jim said.

'We feel the death of Dr Kramer and his two associates are connected,' BJ said. 'We plan to get to the bottom of these murders.'

'I wish you good luck. Murder cases can be tough sometimes, especially if you don't have solid evidence,' Tom warned.

'I can assure you Tom, we will have

solid evidence before prosecuting these murderers,' Jim stated.

'Well, I hope you enjoy our beautiful city,' Tom said, smiling, although he appeared to be quite tense.

'We plan to relax and enjoy our vacation,' Jim said as he stood up and walked to shake Tom's hand. 'It was nice seeing you Tom, and I hope we meet again soon, perhaps in San Diego.'

BJ and I shook Tom's hand, and started to walk out when I turned around and asked Tom, 'By the way, have you ever heard of the name "Madoda"?'

Tom's facial expression changed; he lost his smile and looked puzzled. I must have hit a nerve.

'No, should I know this Madoda?'

'I was just curious. Thanks again.'

As we walked out of Tom's office, I said to Jim and BJ, 'Do you believe any of the nonsense he said about Dr Kramer and his associates being spies and passing secret and sensitive information to foreign governments? And did you see the look on his face when I mentioned Madoda?'

'He looked like he'd seen a ghost,' BJ commented.

'Truly, Frank, I don't believe a word he said. I think he's lying, and did a bad job of hiding it,' Jim said.

'You're right, Jim,' I said. 'I'm now totally convinced that he is involved.'

We drove to a nearby restaurant for a snack. While eating, I felt that we were being watched. I slowly looked around the restaurant.

I took a sip of wine, and as I laid the glass on the table, I said, 'Guys, don't look around, but we're being watched. There are two men sitting by the window. I believe they're FBI agents. Let's finish lunch and leave. We'll see if they follow us.'

I paid the bill, and as we walked out we had a good look of the two men. They were definitely FBI agents; they were following procedures they learned in training. After we drove off, I looked back and saw the two men get into a waiting car and follow us.

'I guess Tom's not wasting any time,' BJ said.

'May I make a suggestion?' I said, 'Why don't we lose these guys, go to the car rental office and change this car. This way we can do our own chasing, and maybe we can come up with something.'

BJ and Jim agreed.

Jim started to drive faster, then he made a sudden right turn into a narrow alley and stopped. The FBI agents did not see us and they sped past the alley. That did it. We finally lost them. We then drove to the car rental office, changed the car, and drove to the hotel. We told Carla, Oliver, Jackie and Rachel what had happened, and that we had to move to another hotel quickly because Tom knew where we were staying. We quickly packed, paid the bill and left the hotel. We drove for about three miles, and found a five-star hotel in a busy area. We checked in.

'While the three of you chase the bad guys, Oliver, Rachel, Jackie, and I will go shopping, OK?' Carla told me.

'Yes darling,' I said. 'But don't forget to get me a present.'

It was time to do our own investigation. We drove to FBI Headquarters and parked in a side street where we could see the FBI garage exit.

Shortly after three o'clock in the afternoon, we saw Tom Collins drive out of the parking garage in a black Mercedes. We followed him, but kept a good distance behind. Tom appeared to be talking on the telephone while driving. He drove towards a suburb of Washington and after ten minutes, he turned into a private dirt road. There was a sign that read, "Private Road - Trespassers Will Be Prosecuted". We slowly followed him anyway. A minute later he stopped his Mercedes in front of a gate. We quickly pulled to the side of the dirt road and then slowly drove over to a grassy area hidden from the road by some trees. We got out of the car and ran towards a concrete wall about four feet high.

Using my tiny binoculars, I saw Tom drive through the gate and stop in front of the entrance to a huge Georgian style building. The building looked like a large hotel, but had armed guards everywhere. There was a big sign on top of the building entrance that read, "The RST Medical Centre".

Two men came out of the building and met Tom. I recognised the two men from the picture in Tom's office. They were Steve Martin and Dr Ramsey Jones.

'I wonder what's going on inside that building?' I asked Jim and BJ. 'And why are the FBI Director, the White House Chief of Staff, and the Secretary of Health meeting secretly here?'

Jim commented, 'I know these three men are very close friends. But meeting in such a place, hidden from the eyes of everyone, protected by armed guards - that looks very suspicious.'

BJ interrupted, 'Do you think this is where they do all their illegal activities? Maybe I should go and pretend I'm visiting a relative, since this place looks like a hospital.'

I looked at BJ and said, 'We don't really know what kind of hospital this is, and besides, who is this relative of yours that is in there? Remember, Tom saw us, or did you forget that fact? They probably have our pictures already, and have warned the guards to watch for us.'

'You're right, Frank,' Jim said, 'And by the way, you told me that Madoda went missing shortly after he was cured of the deadly virus. Do you think he is in there, because if he is, then he is in danger.'

There's only one way to find out,' I said. 'We wait until it gets dark, and then we try to sneak in there and check things out.'

'It's going to be difficult going in there without weapons,' BJ commented.

As we waited for darkness, BJ started to sing, softly, "Yesterday" by the Beatles. He suddenly stopped and said, 'Oh, how I wish for a mature English cheddar cheese sandwich, with tomatoes and onion, smothered with Branston Pickle. And of course, washed down with a pint of bitter.'

We all laughed.

CHAPTER SIXTEEN

It must have been after 8 o'clock and getting dark when we heard a noise not far from us. We hid in the bushes, and few seconds later we saw a figure walking towards us. It was a man, and when he came closer to us we stood up and surrounded him. He was frightened, but not for long. He was neatly dressed with long black trousers, a dark red long sleeve shirt, a sports coat, and black tennis shoes.

'Who are you, and what are you doing here?' I asked him.

He didn't appear to be afraid of us because he looked at us as if he was analysing us. Then he said, 'And who are you, and what are you doing here?'

We didn't answer him. He gave us another look, and he continued, 'I can't see your badges, and you don't belong to the hospital security because if you were, you would have arrested me by now and taken me in.'

I noticed the intruder was carrying a camera, so I asked him, 'Are you a photographer?'

'In a way. I'd better introduce myself. My name is Charlie Still. I am a senior reporter with the Washington Post. When I'm working on a sensitive story, I like to take my own pictures.'

What are you doing here, Mr Still, working on a sensitive story?' I asked him.

Mr Still hesitated for few seconds and then said, 'You keep asking me questions. Maybe first you can tell me who you are.'

I introduced myself and BJ as private investigators from California, and Jim as a friend, who was also the Chief of Police in San Diego.

'So you are doing the same thing I'm doing - investigating,' he commented.

'And what are you investigating, Mr Still?' I asked him.

Mr Still walked around looking at us, then smiled, and said, 'Please call me Charlie.' He paused and then continued, 'I have a hunch about you guys, so I am going to trust you. You seem to be good people and fairly harmless.'

'Well, thank you, Mr Still, sorry Charlie, for sharing your kind thoughts with us. Go on,' I said.

'I've been keeping an eye on this place for over a year. They call it The RST Medical Center; that's R for Ramsey, S for Steve, and T for Tom. These three school buddies own this medical centre, but the public don't know. It's supposed to be a hospital for terminally ill patients, but nobody really knows what's going on inside. Patients are wheeled in, but they never come out. I have a strong suspicion that some sort of research or experiments are being done inside, maybe using human remains, or maybe they are selling human body parts. Who knows.'

'How do you know that? You must know something,' I asked.

Mr Still looked at me and said, 'Then why would they have armed guards all around. Are they hiding something? And who else can keep such a huge place secret? Nobody is going to stand up and question these three powerful men.'

Charlie looked at us as if he was hoping we would agree with him. We were just staring at him, puzzled.

'Charlie,' I said, 'Why don't we go somewhere and talk more about this?'

'I think I'd like that. How about my office?' Charlie suggested.

'That's fine. We'll follow you,' I said.

By the time we arrived at Charlie Still's office, it was after 9 o'clock. Charlie had a large fancy office which led me to believe that he was really what he said he was, a senior reporter.

We were all hungry, so Charlie ordered pizza and soft drinks.

'Something weird is going on in that hospital,' Charlie said. 'I've taken hundreds of pictures of people going in the hospital, but I need to go inside and check it out myself.'

'Can we take a look at the pictures that you took?' I asked Charlie.

Charlie walked to a table in the corner of the room, picked up a box and brought it to us. He opened it, and it was full of pictures. BJ, Jim and I started to look at them, hoping to recognise somebody.

As we looked at the pictures, one of them caught my eyes. It was that of a tall, thin black man being escorted into the hospital by Tom and his two buddies, with two armed guards behind them. It was definitely a picture of Madoda. I recognised him from the picture Dr Kramer had left in his letter to Carla.

I showed the picture to Jim and BJ, then I turned to Charlie and asked him, 'When did you take this picture?'

'About three months ago. I remember this very well. I was wondering why this man was escorted by armed guards. Also, soon after they went inside, they must have gone straight to the top floor. The lights came on and I saw the man looking out of the window. But suddenly someone moved him away from the window and closed the curtains.'

'Do you mind if we keep this picture?' I asked Charlie.

Charlie hesitated for few seconds, then

looked at us and said, 'Look you guys, I've been very cooperative with you, and I have told you what I was doing, but you haven't told me anything about what you are doing here. Yes, you can keep the picture, but tell me, what's going on, maybe we can help each other.'

'I'm getting to that, Charlie,' I said.

As I was about to tell Charlie everything, there was a knock on the door. Charlie opened the door and the security officer handed him two large pizzas and a dozen cans of soft drinks. Charlie spread the pizzas on the table and we all started to eat.

While eating, I turned to Charlie and said, 'We're going to trust you Charlie, but please do not publish or discuss what we are going to tell you with anyone, even your boss, until we finish with our investigation. I promise that you will have the exclusive, agreed?'

'I agree,' Charlie said, raising his right hand and smiling.

'About a month ago, a Dr Kramer, a well-known and respected young scientist, who lived in San Diego with his wife, no children, was killed in a car accident. For some unknown reason no autopsy was done and he was buried. His wife was not even consulted. Recently, his wife came to see me because she suspected that her husband was murdered.

'At the request of Mrs Kramer, and approved by a judge, Jim had Dr Kramer's body exhumed and an autopsy was performed. The autopsy showed that Dr Kramer was poisoned before the accident. Just before he died, Dr Kramer had a meeting with a man in a restaurant. Witnesses could not describe the man he met, other than he was well dressed, wearing a hat and dark glasses, and arrived in a black limousine.'

I paused for a minute while I had a bite of pizza and a sip of Pepsi. Then I continued, 'Now, here's the sensitive part. Dr Kramer and two associates researched and developed a vaccine which could cure a dangerous virus. This virus could quickly spread around the world even if only one person caught it. They filed their complete research data and the vaccine formula in a video tape which Mrs Kramer has. Mrs Kramer insists that her husband was murdered. We believe that whoever killed Dr Kramer wanted this video tape. Also, Dr Kramer's two associates also died in suspicious circumstances: one fell off a cliff while hiking, and the second one was hit by a car as he crossed a street in San Francisco. We believe they were murdered too. Tom Collins sent two of his men to search the Kramer's house on many occasions. We took pictures of these FBI agents while they searched the house. When we visited Tom Collins in his office this morning, he told us that the FBI suspected Dr Kramer might have been a spy and might have passed sensitive secret information to other countries. We really believe that the FBI organisation itself is not involved and has nothing to do with the murders, but Tom and his two buddies have a personal interest to get their hands on the video tape, as it will make them very rich. Can you imagine if these three men owned and controlled the vaccine? Countries all over the world would pay billions of dollars for it.' I then showed Charlie the picture he had given us.

'You see this man? His name is Madoda. He is the man Dr Kramer and his two associates cured from the virus in a village in Zaire, but soon afterwards he disappeared.'

BJ added, 'Madoda is the only living proof that Dr Kramer and his two associates succeeded in their research and developed a vaccine. It appears that our dear FBI Director and his buddies, the White House Chief of Staff and the Secretary of Health, kidnapped Madoda and brought him here for a reason.'

'And we are here to expose these three crooks,' Jim added.

As soon as Jim finished, Charlie said, 'Do you guys know what you are saying? You are accusing three powerful men in the government. This is serious. You then have to ask if the President is involved or knows about this.'

Jim quickly answered, 'I doubt it. These powerful people you refer to, are doing this for their own personal benefit - money. The President is an honest man, and I am sure that he has nothing to do with any of this.'

'What if we see the President and tell him what's going on?' Charlie suggested.

I quickly commented, 'With the Chief of Staff controlling the White House, you won't get within ten feet of the President.'

'Even if we get to the President at this stage, we have no evidence about the murders, or anything,' Jim added.

'I agree with you Jim. We need proof first, then find a way to see the President. Otherwise we're only wasting our time,' I said.

'How about if we sneaked into the hospital and rescued Madoda?' Charlie asked.

'I doubt if we could get anywhere near the building,' BJ said. 'The place looks like a fortress; they have armed guards everywhere. I think we should come up with a better plan. Remember, Tom knows us, so we have to be very careful.'

'There has to be a way. BJ, please call Oliver and tell him to get ready to move out of the hotel with Carla, Jackie and Rachel. We will call him back and tell him which hotel we will be in.'

I turned to Charlie and asked him, 'Charlie, do you know of a good hotel nearby for all of us?'

'I know of an excellent five-star hotel which we use all the time. How many rooms do you want?'

'Six rooms. We need them tonight, like now.'

'I'll reserve them in my name and use my credit card. This way Tom can't trace you. You can depend on the hotel crew; they're reliable and they know how we operate.'

'Thanks a lot, Charlie.'

Charlie made a telephone call and confirmed the reservation. BJ called Oliver again, and gave him the name of the hotel, and told him that we'd see the team in an hour. We then followed Charlie to the hotel. Charlie introduced us to the hotel manager who gave us keys to six rooms on the same floor. Before we went to our rooms, we went to the bar and had a drink while waiting for Oliver and the team to come. They arrived a few minutes later and we all went to our rooms and agreed to meet in the morning for breakfast.

Soon after we went to our room, Carla hugged me and kissed me as if we hadn't seen each other for a month. We undressed and had a shower, and then went to bed for a wonderful love-making session.

CHAPTER SEVENTEEN

When I woke up at 8 o'clock in the morning, I looked out of the window and saw the sun was shining and the sky was blue. Carla was already dressed looking as beautiful as ever. I had her in my arms and we were kissing when there was knock at the door. I opened the door and without an invitation the team came in, followed by Jim.

'Well, it's nice to see everybody here. Shall we go and have breakfast?'

'We were going to have breakfast without you, knowing you would be busy,' Rachel said smiling while looking at Carla.

The breakfast looked like lunch, there was so much to eat. While eating I explained to everybody what had happened and told them about our meeting with Charlie. As soon as we finished we went upstairs to my room. Charlie came in just as we were about to discuss the situation. I introduced him to my team, and he appeared impressed, and said, 'Where on earth do you find such beautiful girls, Frank? Maybe I should join your team.' Everybody laughed. Charlie then told me that he had an appointment and needed to go, but would be back later. After Charlie left, I turned and started the discussion.

'Now that you know the situation, we need to find a way to get into the medical centre for two reasons: First, we must find the main office and hide a couple of cameras because we need some hard evidence if we ever have to bring these people to justice. And second, we must find Madoda and get him out of there.'

'Before we start,' Carla said as she pulled a video tape from her bag and handed it to me.

'Thank you Carla,' I said, 'and now, any ideas about how we could get in there?'

'Whatever we do, it has to be convincing. We don't want them to suspect us in any way,' Jim added.

There was silence in the room when suddenly BJ said, 'I've got it. Tom saw three of us, so we can't get into the RST Medical Center. But he didn't see Oliver and Rachel. What if Oliver and Rachel visit the medical centre and pretend to be a wealthy couple from France whose 12-year old son has been infected with a new mysterious disease. They are now in America looking for the best hospital to cure their son.'

Everybody was quiet, thinking and looking at each other. After a minute of silence, I commented, 'That's an excellent idea, BJ. Let's discuss it further.'

'And while inside, they will probably take you to meet the man in charge of the whole operation. That's where you can find a way to hide the tiny recorders/cameras,' Jackie said.

'But, how are they going to convince Tom and his two buddies to admit their son?' Jim asked.

'Money,' BJ said.

'You mean offer them a large sum of money if they cure their son?' I asked.

'Yes, money always talks,' BJ replied. 'Oliver and Rachel could offer them a deposit, say $100,000, and tell them that if they cure their son, they will give them an additional $900,000. But Oliver and Rachel must insist they meet with the owners of the medical centre and the doctor in charge before they give them any money.'

'With that much money, I am sure they will accept,' Jackie said.

'Except for one thing,' BJ said, showing a wide grin, 'can Rachel and Oliver speak French?'

'Of course we can,' Oliver replied. Oliver then stood up, walked to Rachel, and spoke to her in French, 'Bonsoir, Mademoiselle, voulez-vous danser? meaning, "Good evening, Miss, would you like to dance?"'

And Rachel replied in French, 'Oui, avec plaisir! meaning, "Yes, with pleasure!"'

Everybody laughed, while Rachel said, 'I learned French in school, and Oliver lived in France for few years with his parents.'

As I walked around the room, and thought about BJ's suggestion, I became convinced that it was an excellent plan. To ensure that everybody heard the plan correctly, I started to review it, 'Let me see if I've got this right. Rachel and Oliver will visit the medical centre, driven in a fancy limousine. They pretend to be a wealthy French couple looking for a hospital to treat their only son who is infected with a deadly virus. They meet the person in charge and explain the purpose of their visit, and while doing that, somehow Rachel must find a way to hide the two cameras. Then when they meet the three buddies, the camera rolls, and we get them on tape. I like it.'

'Now that we've solved the language problem, we have another problem,' BJ said. 'Who's going to be the driver of the limousine?'

'How about Charlie Still?' Jim suggested.

I thought about what Jim said. Since Tom already knew about us, using Charlie as the driver was our only solution, if he accepted the task. I called Charlie and asked him to meet us that night at the hotel restaurant.

'Well, let's take a rest this afternoon and meet tonight for supper,' I suggested.

Carla and I went to our room. As soon as we entered we hugged each other and kissed. Still hugging each other, I carried Carla to the bed, kissing and slowly undressing until we were both naked. And we indulged in passionate love. It was beautiful, we never wanted it to end.

We were all at the bar later having a drink when Charlie came in. As Charlie sat down, I said, 'Charlie, I'd like to ask you two favours. First, we need a limousine and a van, and we need them the day after tomorrow. We also need some electronic equipment. Jackie and Rachel will fill you in. Can you arrange for all that?'

'Of course I can. And what's the second favour?' Charlie asked.

I briefed Charlie about our plan. I told him we would like him to be the chauffeur. He accepted, and he liked our plan. I asked him to meet us on Friday morning at 11 o'clock outside the hotel.

Our table was ready, so we moved into the dining room. We had a wonderful meal; lobster and all the trimmings, and of course lot of wine.

When we finished dinner, I whispered in Carla's ear, then we both stood up, and I said, 'That was a delicious meal. Carla and I will take a walk. Tomorrow you'll be busy working on the plan for the exciting day after, so I'll leave you to it, and Carla and I will go sightseeing.'

It must have been after 10 o'clock when Carla and I left the restaurant. I felt I was the happiest man in the world having Carla beside me. Here I was at last, with my beautiful Blue Eyes, my only love, the one I had been dreaming about for over six years. I loved her and I would never let her go again.

We walked holding hands, and every now and then we would stop and kiss. We entered a park and sat on a bench. Carla sat on my lap and hugged me.

I thought it was the right time to tell Carla what I always wanted to tell her. I gently put my fingers under her chin, and faced her saying, 'Carla, I want to marry you as soon as we get back to San Diego.'

Carla looked very happy, and with a big smile she hugged me and said, 'Yes darling. I will marry you.' She hugged me tight and kissed me, and then laid her head on my shoulder.

We returned to the hotel around midnight. We didn't turn the lights on. We undressed and went straight to bed, and made love. We were like a ball of fire.

As we laid naked in bed, Carla said, 'Darling, I have a wonderful surprise gift for you for our wedding. You'll love it.'

'Can't you tell me now, please, darling?' I begged her.

'No, I can't. It won't be surprise if I tell you now. You'll just have to wait.'

CHAPTER EIGHTEEN

The next morning we went to the bank with a briefcase and withdrew $100,000, all in $100 dollar bills. We stacked them in the briefcase and went back to the hotel. At the hotel we put the money in the hotel safety deposit room. Carla and I had lunch, and then we went to visit some of Washington's beautiful attractions and we did some shopping and then returned to the hotel. We were exhausted, so I ordered two drinks and we sat by the pool.

Friday morning started very well: it was sunny and warm, but the weatherman said on TV that there would be some drizzle in the evening, and plenty of rain in the days ahead.

Charlie was waiting outside the hotel with the limousine when Oliver and Rachel came out. They looked great: dressed as a fashionable rich French couple, and Charlie was dressed like a top class chauffeur.

I approached them and asked, 'Do you have everything you need?'

And in French, Oliver answered, 'Oui, Monsieur, meaning "Yes, Sir". Let's get the show on the road.'

'Remember,' I told Oliver, 'You must find a way for Rachel to hide the cameras and recorders. If anything goes wrong, let us know somehow. We'll be outside.'

The three of them were wired, so they could hear us and we could hear them. Charlie drove the limousine, while Jim, BJ, Jackie, Carla and I followed in the van a short distance behind.

As we approached the medical centre, we slowed down and pulled off the road into our usual spot while the limousine continued towards the gate. We got out of the van and walked to the perimeter wall where we had a clear view of the medical centre.

The armed guards allowed the limousine to drive through the gate after Oliver told them that they were there to meet the man in charge of the medical centre. Oliver saw the guard he spoke to calling someone on the phone.

A well-dressed man welcomed Oliver and Rachel at the entrance door and escorted them inside, while Charlie stayed by the limousine. We rushed back to the van and turned on the monitor, waiting for Rachel to install the camera and recorder.

Inside the building, Oliver and Rachel were taken to an office to meet the man in charge. The man stood up and welcomed them, saying, 'I am Mr Scott, and I am in charge of the RST Medical Center. Please have a seat.'

As soon as Oliver and Rachel sat down, Oliver spoke with a French accent, 'I am Maurice Olivier, and this is my wife, Rachel.'

'I'm pleased to meet you Mr and Mrs Olivier, how can I help you?' Mr Scott asked.

Oliver was quick to answer, 'I would like to thank you for allowing us to meet with you. Although we didn't have an appointment, we decided to come anyway because we were anxious to discuss our problem with you. It's an urgent problem that needs to be resolved quickly. We heard you have the best medical facility in the United States, so we decided to come over and ask you to treat our son. If you succeed in treating him, we will pay you generously.'

'Of course, we will do our best to help you, but tell me please, what is the problem with your son?'

Oliver started telling Mr Scott the story we agreed to tell them. 'A little over a year ago, our 12-year old son, Pierre, had an operation in Paris. Unfortunately, there were complications, and he needed blood. But the blood they gave him was infected with a bad and deadly virus. We could have sued that hospital for all they had, but what would that do? It will not bring my Pierre's health back. The hospital agreed to pay for all medical expenses in order to cure our son. So you see Mr Scott, we are willing to pay your hospital $100,000 in cash as an initial payment, and a remaining $900,000 when Pierre has fully recovered. Would that be agreeable to you?'

With his eyes wide open, showing signs of excitement, Mr Scott said, 'Of course, that would be fine. I will discuss this with the owners of the medical centre and the doctor in charge. When would you like to bring your son, Mr Olivier?'

'As soon as possible, Mr Scott,' Oliver replied. 'When you discuss it with your staff, and give us a written agreement, we will bring you the deposit of $100,000. But we would like to personally meet the owners of this medical centre and also the doctor who will look after our son. We have only one son, and we have to make sure he will be taken care of. You see, Mr Scott, $1,000,000 is a lot of money, so we need the best medical treatment.'

Mr Scott quickly replied, 'Oh yes, I can guarantee your son will receive the best treatment. The owners and the doctor could meet you and discuss all the details. How about the day after tomorrow, Sunday? Could you come at 10 o'clock in the morning?'

'That would be good, Mr Scott.'

At this moment, Rachel started to cough loudly. Oliver looked at Mr Scott and said, 'My wife has a very bad sinus problem. I wonder if you have a bottle of water, but it has to be Perrier; that's the only water she drinks. Please, hurry up.'

Mr Scott jumped up. 'I'll go and see if we have Perrier water. I'll be right back.' He ran out of the room.

As soon as Mr Scott left the room, Rachel went to work while Oliver waited by the door watching for Mr Scott. Rachel quickly opened the air conditioning vents, one on the wall facing the desk, and the other behind the desk, and placed a small camera and a recorder in each of them.

Mr Scott must have had difficulty finding the Perrier. That gave Rachel more time to set the cameras in place and make sure they were working properly. She called the van, and they answered, and were able to check that the feed was functioning well. Rachel was happy that they were working, and she closed the vents. As soon as Oliver saw Mr Scott coming, he alerted Rachel, and she started to cough as Mr Scott came in. Rachel drank the water, and her coughing stopped.

'I hope you feel better, Mrs Olivier.'

'Much better, Mr Scott. Thank you.'

'Well, I would like to assure you that if you bring your son here, we would do our best to cure him.'

'I'll take you at your word Mr Scott. We'll see you on Sunday with the $100,000. It is very important that we meet the owners and the doctor who will be treating our son. We want to be very careful about who treats our son. The doctors who looked after Pierre in Paris were just quacks in white uniforms. I guess you find doctors like that in any country.'

'I assure you we are professionals, and we specialise in difficult medical problems. Our doctors are experts in the area of curing such viruses,' Mr Scott assured us.

'By the way, if your medical centre can't treat our son, please let us know as soon as possible, so we can go somewhere else,' Oliver stressed to Mr Scott.

'Don't worry, sir. We'll see you on Sunday,' Mr Scott replied as he escorted Oliver and Rachel to the limousine. He then shook their hands, and bid them goodbye as they drove off.

Charlie drove the limousine to where the van was, and we all gathered to see the result of Rachel's hard work. As we looked at the two monitors, we saw Mr Scott return to his office, and make a telephone call. The camera behind the desk showed the number he dialled. It was Tom's number at FBI Headquarters.

'Tom, hi, this is Scott. I just had a visit from a French couple. They must be very rich. They have a son who's dying of the virus. They want us to treat him, and they are willing to give us $100,000 cash as initial payment, and $900,000 when their son is cured. They will come here on Sunday with the money. But they insisted on meeting the owners of the medical centre and the doctor before they bring their son for treatment, otherwise they'll go somewhere else.'

(There was a pause - Tom was talking.)

Mr Scott continued, 'Don't worry Tom, they're French. They will probably drop their son off and then go back to France. So why don't you, Steve, and Doc Ramsey come over on Sunday, before 10 o'clock in the morning, and meet this couple. That's a lot of money, Tom.'

(There was a pause - Tom was talking.)

'Why don't we experiment on the son, maybe use some of Madoda's blood for transfusion. If it doesn't work and he dies, then we can bury the son and the couple somewhere, just like we did with that rich couple from Canada last year. Nobody will ever find them. And at least we'll get the $100,000 in cash.

After a short pause, Mr Scott said, 'Ok Tom, I'll see the three of you on Sunday.'

After Mr Scott finished talking with Tom, he rested his back on the leather chair, put his legs on the desk, and lit a cigar, with a grin in his face.

I looked at Rachel and Oliver and said, 'You guys did a super job.'

'Everything we saw and Mr Scott's conversation are on tape,' Rachel said, and added, 'That in itself will incriminate them. And by the way, as we were walking out with Mr Scott we passed a room with a small window. I looked inside and saw a tall black man. I didn't think much about it at the time, but I now believe it was Madoda.'

'I agree with you Rachel. They probably kidnapped him and brought him here. They will probably kill him when they finish.' I looked at the team and I said, 'Great, it has been a long day, let's go back to the hotel, and work on Sunday's plan.'

Back at the hotel, we all gathered in my room.

'So far, it looks like they fell for it,' BJ commented.

'And we know that Madoda is in there. We have to rescue him,' Jim declared.

'That's why we have to plan the next step with caution because what's in those tapes will be our only evidence against them,' I said.

'You are absolutely right Frank,' Jim said, 'As soon as we gather enough solid evidence that incriminates them, then we go in for a search and get the tapes. We need solid evidence. Let's hope they don't find the tapes.'

'It will also give me good pictures for the exclusive,' Charlie commented with a grin on his face.

BJ suggested, 'How about Oliver and Rachel go to the medical centre at 10:30 on Sunday, instead of 10 o'clock. That way the three partners will be in the room, and they will have time to talk about their business while waiting. The more we have on tape the better.'

'I like that,' I said. 'Well, it seems that we will have a busy day on Sunday. Enjoy yourselves tomorrow; go shopping, tour Washington or whatever. And why don't we meet tomorrow night for dinner in the hotel restaurant, say around 7. Then we can go to my room and go over our plan for Sunday.'

'That's a good idea,' Jim said. 'I do have to meet an old friend of mine, if he has the time to see me; he is a very busy man. Anyway, see you tomorrow night.'

As Jim walked out of the room, BJ looked at me and asked, 'And what are you planning to do?'

'Oh, Carla and I have a lot of planning and catching up to do, so you can all go and enjoy yourselves.' Putting my arm on Charlie's shoulder, I continued, 'Charlie here knows Washington inside out, and he will show you a good time.'

I opened the door to give them the hint. It worked; they looked at each other, then Jackie said as she was walking out, 'Let's go and have dinner, and then boogie all night.'

Rachel agreed, 'Well, I haven't been jogging for two days, so some dancing would do me a lot of good. Let's go.'

As soon as they left, I pulled Carla to me and we kissed. The next I knew, we were in bed making love. Our love was becoming stronger and stronger. We wanted to be together all the time; we wanted to be part of each other.

We didn't go out that night. We had dinner in the room, and then ended up in bed again. In between, I looked at Carla and said, 'You have a wonderful body, and it's delicious too.' And our naked bodies were glued together again.

It was after midnight, and we were still awake. We sat on the balcony, Carla sitting on my lap, resting her head on my shoulder. She appeared comfortable and safe.

Looking at her face and her desirable lips, I couldn't resist but kissed her lips gently as I said, 'Carla, I love you more than anything in this world, and I don't know how I would survive without you.' I started to kiss every part of her body, and she was enjoying it. She couldn't resist it any more, she was yearning for more love - and I was too. There was no end to our lovemaking.

Carla looked at me, with her beautiful sparkling blue eyes, and said, in a soft voice, 'I told you this before, and I want to keep saying it. I fell in love with you the moment I saw you at Gallal's shop. I am just sorry I didn't come back to you six years ago. So much time wasted. But now that we are together, I will never leave you. You are my life.'

She kissed me and laid her head on my bare chest, and we both fell asleep.

CHAPTER NINETEEN

The next morning I woke up before Carla. I enjoy waking up early in the morning; it's a habit from my days in Cairo. Unfortunately, there were no mosques and no prayers by the Muezzin here.

I called the restaurant and ordered breakfast. I looked out of the window and saw the sky was cloudy and dull, rain was on the horizon. Still gazing outside, I thought of Jim, and I wondered who he was going to see today. He never told me he had a friend in Washington DC.

Carla slowly came behind me, put her hands on my bare chest and kissed my back. I turned around and our lips met, and we kissed passionately. We were interrupted by a knock on the door. It was breakfast.

Picking up some bacon and a piece of bread, she said, 'I'm starving. Let's eat and then go out and explore.'

I looked at her and smiled, 'Anything you want, my Blue Eyes.'

We spent the day visiting many of the attractions in Washington and getting wet. It was late afternoon when we went back to the hotel. We had an intimate shower, rested for two hours, and then went to meet the team at the bar.

'Did you enjoy yourselves last night?' I asked.

'You can say that again. I've never danced so much in my life. My feet are killing me,' Jackie said.

Looking at Charlie, Rachel said, 'And Charlie here is an excellent dancer and he wouldn't stop. He kept us hopping all night.'

'If you stayed in DC, you wouldn't need to jog anymore, just dance,' Charlie commented.

We moved to the dining room. I could see Jackie and Rachel had difficulty walking, and they looked tired. After we finished dinner we agreed to meet in front of the hotel around 10 o'clock in the morning.

Carla and I went for a walk, and then back to the hotel. I had ordered champagne earlier and it was waiting for us when we returned to the room.

Another night of lovemaking was on the horizon.

Dark clouds covered the sky on Sunday morning. We all met in front of the hotel. I handed Oliver the briefcase containing $100,000 in $100 bills. Since this might be dangerous, and guards might shoot at us, I gave everybody a gun and a box of bullets. I told all of them, 'Talking with Jim, he suggested you carry a gun for self-defence. He knows about the guns and he approved them. Jim has his own police gun.

Also,' I said, 'you are all wired, just in case something goes wrong with the cameras. We will be watching you when you go inside, and remember, if you find yourself in any danger, protect yourself first and then tell us. We will only be seconds away from you.'

Looking at Jim, I asked him, 'Did you meet your friend yesterday?'

'Oh yes, he was so thrilled to see me. We were close buddies in college, just like brothers.'

Before leaving I said to Jim, 'Maybe I can meet him sometime.'

'Yes, you will. I told him about you, and he wants to meet you.'

I put my arms around Oliver and Rachel and I said, 'We'll leave now to go to our spot. Charlie, wait for about 15 minutes after we leave, then drive straight to the gate. Don't stop at our spot.'

'Don't worry boss,' Oliver said, 'We'll be fine.'

'And by the way, Oliver, when you leave the medical centre, drive straight to the hotel. Don't stop at our usual spot. Just be careful.'

We drove the van to our lay by. It was just around 10 o'clock when we saw Tom Collins, Steve Martin and Dr Ramsey Jones arrive in a Mercedes. Tom was driving. We hid behind the van.

'Hurry up Jackie, turn on the cameras,' I said.

Jackie quickly went into the van and turned on the cameras. We joined her, and stood around the monitors and watched. It wasn't long before we saw the three buddies enter the room, followed by Mr Scott.

'So you say this couple is French?' Tom asked Scott.

'Yes, they are so worried about their son, they would give anything to see him get well.'

Turning to Ramsey, Tom asked, 'We know very well that we cannot cure their son because we don't have the formula. We need to get that video tape soon. But is there anything we can do to show them that we could cure their son?'

'We can only do our best. Remember, we tried to cure those two guys from Canada, but unfortunately it didn't work and they died. We had to cremate them.'

After a short pause, Ramsey asked Steve, 'Maybe we can use their son in a new experiment. I was thinking about this, what do you think?'

'What kind of experiment are we talking about?' Tom asked.

'Well, we could take blood from Madoda and inject it into their son. We could do that few times a week. Although we don't have the video tape and the vaccine formula, maybe that would work. And if it doesn't work we kill the parents and the son just like we killed all the others.'

Steve stood up, and in an irritable loud voice, he said, 'How much blood can we extract from Madoda, and how do we know the blood would save him? I don't think it will work. I told you we should never have killed Dr Kramer and his two associates until we had the video tape in our hands.'

Tom shouted back, 'Steve, you forget Dr Kramer threatened to expose us. Do you want to spend the rest of your life behind bars? Well, I don't. It's just a matter of time and we will get the video tape. Mrs Kramer will give it to us, with some persuasion.'

Dr Jones appeared to be thinking. He turned to Steve and said, in a convincing voice, 'Tom is right, Steve. Now, let's not argue about this. Once we get that video tape, it's like treasure. We will all be multi-millionaires. Don't forget that. Just be patient.'

'Don't worry, Steve,' Tom said, trying to calm him. 'We know Mrs Kramer has the video tape, and sooner or later we will get it from her. I say again, Steve, relax.'

'But what if this kid dies, how can we explain it to the parents?' Steve asked.

'Like we agreed before,' Ramsey said, 'We'll have to dispose of the parents too - after we get the money, and if anybody asks about them, we can say we never heard of them.'

To reassure Steve, Tom said, 'We would have to get rid of the chauffeur too. This way we make sure nobody knows anything. We will cremate all of them. Are you happy with that, Steve?'

'Yes, I'm happy. I think we should insist the parents pay us the remaining $900,000 (or at least half that) when they admit their son, just in case something goes wrong.'

Ramsey smiled and said, 'If they are so anxious to cure their only son, they will most probably agree to pay. We have to convince them.'

'And that we will do,' Tom smiled too.

The telephone rang as Tom was talking. Scott answered the call and after few seconds, he hung up and said, 'The French couple just came in, so let's put on our caring voices and welcome them.'

The limousine was about to stop in front of the entrance when Tom, Steve, Ramsey, and Scott came out. Oliver and Rachel stepped out of the limousine. They were greeted by Scott who introduced them to Tom, Steve, and Ramsey. They all entered the medical centre. Oliver carried the briefcase containing the $100,000.

BJ, Jim, Jackie and myself watched and heard everything the trio said. That was enough to put them in jail for the rest of their lives. I commented, 'Everything seems to be going as planned; we have the evidence, now we have to work on getting them out, with Madoda.'

Tom escorted Oliver and Rachel to his office, and as they sat down, Tom said, 'We are glad you decided to have your only son treated in our hospital, Mr Olivier. Dr Jones here is the best when it comes to treating virus cases like this. You can rest assured we will take good care of your son.'

In a posh French accent, Oliver said, 'I would like to repeat what I told Mr Scott. Our son's health is most important. We want him cured and we don't want him to die.'

Rachel pretended to cry. Oliver walked to her and put his arms around her shoulder saying, 'Please darling, don't cry. I am sure these gentlemen will take good care of Pierre.'

Then turning to the men, Oliver said, 'You see gentleman, my wife loves Pierre.

He is the only son we have, and she cannot conceive any more children. Now how long do you think it will take to cure him?'

Dr Jones replied, 'Not long, around eight to ten weeks. But your son's treatment will be quite complex and will require a lot of special care and attention. That is very expensive.' He then walked closer to Oliver and Rachel and said, 'We are treating a number of other men who have a similar diagnosis. They have been here for over ten weeks, but they are getting better. Since you came all the way from France, we will have to treat your son ahead of the other patients. So, the $100,000 you plan to give us today is just enough to start the treatment. To ensure your son is well taken care of, and completely cured as soon as possible, I suggest you pay the remaining $900,000 when you admit your son. Would you agree to that?'

Oliver paused for a minute and then whispered at Rachel's ear. He then turned to Dr Ramsey and said, 'I guess we have no choice and we have to trust you. Our son will arrive from Paris tomorrow afternoon. We will bring him here directly from the airport.'

Tom said, 'We will be waiting for Pierre.'

'Here is the $100,000 initial payment. Could you please give me a receipt.' Oliver handed the case to Ramsey. Ramsey opened the case and saw the money: $100,000 stacked in $100 bills. He looked at the others and smiled.

'Of course, the receipt,' Ramsey said. He opened the desk drawer and brought a blank sheet of paper. He wrote on it, 'Received $100,000 from Mr Olivier as an initial payment for treatment of his son. Mr Olivier will pay us the final payment of $900,000 upon admitting his son for treatment.' Ramsey signed the receipt and gave it to Oliver, saying, 'Don't worry Mr Olivier. Bring your son tomorrow when he arrives from France and we will take care of him.'

'Thank you gentlemen, thank you very much. We have to leave now to get the $900,000 from our bank. See you tomorrow,' Oliver said.

While Scott escorted Oliver and Rachel to the limousine, Tom looked out of the window. As Charlie opened the door for Oliver and Rachel to get in, he turned his head towards Tom. Tom suddenly looked at Steve and Ramsey, and asked them to hurry up to the window where he was standing. When they approached the window, Tom pointed his finger towards the limousine.

'You see that chauffeur,' Tom said, 'he's familiar. I have a feeling I've seen him before, but I can't remember where.'

A few seconds passed, and suddenly Tom snapped his fingers and said, 'Now I remember. He's a reporter with the Washington Post. He used to attend the President's press conferences. I saw him there. I have a feeling we're being set up.'

'How can you be sure? I don't remember seeing him before, and I'm the White House Chief of Staff,' Steve remarked.

'Then why would a reporter act as a chauffeur, you tell me,' Tom asked.

'Maybe you are confusing him with someone else,' Steve replied. He continued, 'You assume this couple are not really who they say they are. Then why did they give us $100,000 in cash? Are they crazy?'

Ramsey was not happy with the discussion, so he said, 'If they don't bring their son and the $900,000 tomorrow, then we'll know something is wrong. So instead of bickering, let us wait until tomorrow, OK?'

Scott came back into the room, and Tom told him what he thought of the chauffeur.

Tom looked unhappy, and said, 'I don't know. I'm not comfortable. We don't want to take chances. So to be extra careful, I suggest we bring in more guards tomorrow. If the Oliviers turn out to be fake, we will have to dispose of them, and their chauffeur as well. We worked hard to get where we are now, so let us keep it that way.

Before the three buddies left, Scott assured them, 'I will personally make sure we have plenty of guards tomorrow, so don't worry.'

We saw and heard what they said. Everything was also documented on the tape, so we had to retrieve the two tapes from the room as they contained solid evidence to put the group away for a long time.

Back in my hotel room, BJ was concerned,

'Those guys really mean business. They are dangerous.'

Jackie was quick to add, 'I have this strong feeling that if Oliver, Rachel, and Charlie go there tomorrow, they will be in grave danger. They might get killed.'

'Yes, I know, and that worries me.' I said as I turned to Jim. 'Well Jim, you are the maestro in this area, how do you think we should handle this situation, any ideas?'

Jackie was furious, 'But we cannot take a chance. These are vicious killers. You heard what they said. They plan to have more armed guards.'

'I have to agree with Jackie,' Jim commented. 'Rachel and Oliver inside, held in a room, and Charlie outside surrounded by armed guards - they will definitely be in danger. And like BJ said, they are really dangerous. But on the other hand, we have no case without those tapes. We have no choice but to find a way to get in there, get the tapes, and rescue Madoda.'

'Why don't we take BJ with us tomorrow, I mean hide him in the trunk of the limousine?' Charlie suggested. 'That way he's inside the gate in case we need him. If things get out of hand, call the cops, then come in and help us.'

'It might take time for the cops to get there, and by that time it might be too late, and we'll all be dead,' Rachel said.

'I know the Chief of Police here in DC. I met him few years ago when we were working on a case. I'll have a word with him and explain the situation. I'll ask him to stay close by with his men in case we need them,' Jim suggested.

I looked at Jim with surprise, and said, 'I didn't know you had a friend in the Police Department here, but it is a good idea. We will need all the help we can get.'

I looked at everybody and said, 'Well, let's get ready for tomorrow.'

'We'll need to be ready to go at two o'clock in the afternoon,' BJ reminded everybody.

After everybody left, I hugged Carla, 'Carla, I'm really worried about tomorrow. There might be shooting, and we could be in danger, so I would like you to stay in the hotel until we get back. Things might get tough out there, and I can't risk having you there.'

'No, Frank. Remember I said I will always be with you, so I want to go with you. Please,' Carla begged.

I paused to think, and then said, 'OK, you can come but you must promise me that you will stay in the van at all times. There might be shooting. Agree?'

'Yes, I agree my darling. But now I want you, your lips, your body, and your love.'

CHAPTER TWENTY

As we prepared to leave the hotel the next day, the sky was dark and it was raining heavily, with thunder and lightning circling us ominously.

The limousine and the van stopped in the usual spot near the medical centre. BJ hid inside the trunk of the limousine. Charlie drove towards the gate. The guards were waiting for them, and waved them through. As they parked near the entrance, Mr Scott ran towards the limousine with an open umbrella and escorted them to the building.

Jim, Carla, Jackie and myself went inside the back of the van. Jackie turned on the cameras while we gathered around and watched the monitors. We waited for few minutes and then saw Oliver, Rachel and

Scott enter the office. Tom welcomed them, 'Nice to see you again, but where's your son?'

'We apologise, Messieurs,' Oliver said, 'he was not feeling good, so the doctors in Paris suggested we wait a few more days before he could travel.'

Tom walked slowly towards the desk, and then turned around with a gun in his hand. 'Now, dear Mr and Mrs Olivier, who are you, and what do you want here?'

Steve and Ramsey stood by Tom, with guns in their hands also.

'You'd better explain or you are both dead, and your chauffeur too,' Steve said aggressively.

Oliver stood in front of Rachel with his hands raised, and said, 'Listen you guys, we are just trying to get you treat our son.'

'You're lying,' Ramsey shouted. 'You just spoke with an American accent. What happened to your French accent?'

Tom moved closer to us, still pointing his gun, and said, 'You'd better tell us who you work for, quick, or I'll shoot both of you here right now.'

Oliver thought of the situation they were in, and decided to stall them until we were able to get into the compound and help them.

'Ok, I'll tell you the truth,' Oliver said, taking his time. 'Mrs Kramer, wife of Dr Kramer, you know who I am talking about, the one you guys killed together with his two associates, well, she asked us to come here and find out why you killed the three of them.

'So you know about that,' Tom said. 'Yes, we killed them, and unfortunately for you, we are going to make sure you join them, and nobody will know what we did.'

'And then we will take care of Mrs Kramer after she gives us the video tape,' Steve added.

Tom pointed his gun at Oliver, but Oliver quickly raised his hands up and said, 'Wait! If I can get you this video tape that you're after, would you let us go free? We are only hired to do a job. It is not worth killing the three of us, and then Mrs Kramer. So what do you think?'

I was watching the monitors, and I knew Oliver was trying to buy us time. So I called Charlie; he was outside by the limousine waiting for Rachel and Oliver. 'Charlie, Oliver and Rachel are in grave danger. Get BJ out of the trunk and be ready. We're on our way.'

Charlie went to the trunk, opened it and got BJ out, saying, 'Let's just wait here.'

Just as we were about to drive the van towards the medical centre, Jim made a telephone call.

'What was that about?' I asked Jim.

'Calling the cavalry,' Jim replied with a smile.

At the same time, Tom, Steve, and Ramsey were quietly discussing what Oliver had told them. Ramsey turned to Oliver and said, 'So explain this to me. Why would you give us $100,000 in cash? There is more to this than what you are telling us.'

'I think you are lying Mr Olivier,' Steve added. 'You have one minute to tell us or you are both dead.'

It was still raining heavily with claps of thunder, and dark clouds covered the sky. We drove the van to the gate and the security guards stopped us.

'We were called to fix a leak in the room of the boss, the rain must have damaged the roof,' I told the armed guard.

'I have no record of roof damage, so you just turn around and drive off.' The guard spoke in a firm voice and pointed his gun at us, and again ordered us to drive off.

I backed the van for about 20 feet as if I was leaving, but instead of leaving, I drove towards the gate at high speed. The guards started to shoot at the van. I braked as the van came parallel with the limousine, and told Jackie to stay in the van with Carla. Jim and I quickly exited the van and joined Charlie and BJ.

It appears that when Tom and his buddies heard the sound of the shooting, they ran to the window to see what was happening. At the same time, Oliver and Rachel took advantage of the distraction; they turned the lights off and ran out of the room. Tom, Steve, Ramsey and Scott started to shoot towards the door.

Outside the door, Oliver and Rachel pulled their guns out and saw two guards running towards them, shooting. Oliver and Rachel fired back and both guards went down. Tom, Steve, Ramsey and Scott remained in the room, and made a telephone call asking for more guards to come. More guards started to come from both sides of the hallway. Oliver and Rachel kept firing in both directions. They appeared to be pinned down, and couldn't move in either direction.

We were hiding between the limousine and the van, exchanging shots with the guards. More guards kept coming and shooting at us, and we were shooting back. Oliver and Rachel were still in the building.

The rain was getting heavier and the wind was getting stronger.

'I'm going in,' I told Jim. 'It's taking Oliver and Rachel a long time to come out. Something must have happened to them.'

'Be careful, Frank,' Jim said. 'We'll cover you.'

Jim, BJ, and Charlie were shooting in opposite directions as more guards kept coming towards us and shooting. But when I looked behind me towards the gate, I saw bunch of men rushing towards us while shooting at the guards.

One of them dived past me and said, 'We're the FBI, the good ones.'

I looked at him and smiled saying, 'Thanks. Glad you're here. Now I have to go inside the building because two of my people are pinned down in there. You guys cover me.'

The FBI agent who appeared to be in charge, shouted at his men, 'Cover him and go with him into the building.'

As I ran towards the building, everybody started shooting in all directions. I saw Oliver on the floor immediately inside the building entrance. He was shot in the leg. Rachel was shooting at the guards and pulling Oliver to one side. I told the FBI agents following me to cover her and to help Oliver outside.

I knelt beside Oliver and asked him, 'Can you make it?'

'Yes, I can. Let's get out of here.'

Two of the FBI agents helped Oliver who leant on their shoulders, and slowly walked him out covered by other FBI agents. Rachel was also accompanied by FBI agents. I stayed by the door and kept firing at the guards to hold them inside the building.

Rain was pouring down even more heavily, with thunder and lightning adding to the drama. I was at the door when I saw Oliver and Rachel safely reach the van.

I didn't see Tom looking out of the window with a gun in his hand. I was about 20 feet from the van as Tom aimed to shoot at me.

Carla saw him, and she quickly ran out of the van towards me, shouting, 'Frank, Frank, look out.' I turned around as Carla threw herself at me at the same time that Tom fired.

BJ turned towards the window, and fired repeatedly at Tom. Tom went down.

I was kneeling on the wet ground holding onto Carla. I knew she was shot, the shot that was meant for me. Her eyes slightly open, she looked at me and said, 'Are you alright, Frank?'

Carla was in pain. Tears were pouring down my face as I said, 'Yes darling, I'm OK. Why didn't you stay in the van?'

'I had to warn you, darling,' Carla spoke slowly, her head resting on my arms.

I hugged Carla and I didn't want her to go. She was my life. I couldn't live without her. I needed her and I loved her so much.

The paramedics gently took Carla from my arms and put her on a stretcher, covered her and took her away. Jackie and Rachel helped me off the ground, both hugging me and crying.

As I looked around, I saw another stretcher with a covered body on it. It was Tom. I also saw Steve, Ramsey, and Scott handcuffed and taken away by the FBI.

'Did you get the tapes from Tom's office?'
I asked BJ.

'Yes, we did,' replied BJ.

'And Madoda, is he safe?'

'Yes, he's safe and in good hands. Now, Frank, let us go.

It was still raining heavily when we drove to the hospital to check on Oliver's leg. The doctor removed the bullet from his leg and assured us that he would recover soon. He commiserated about Carla.

We then returned to the hotel.

I felt lonely and sick as I entered my room. All I could think of was Carla, and all I could see around me was Carla. How could I live without her? I had just lost the only girl I ever loved, my only love. I sat at the corner of the bed with my head down and I cried. My heart was beating hard. I couldn't control myself. I was crying like a little child. I felt my insides tearing to pieces. I wished I was dead because I wanted to be with Carla.

I heard a knock on the door, but I ignored it. After a few seconds the door opened and I saw Jim come in. I didn't say a word. He knew what I was going through. He sat by me, put his arms around my shoulders, and said, 'The manager gave me a key to your door, so I thought of talking to you before I go to bed.' Jim paused for few seconds, then said, ' Frank, do you remember I told you about my Martha? I worshipped her and I loved her more than anything in the world. When she died, I felt I was finished. I wanted to kill myself. I desperately wanted to be with her. I thought I might as well be with her in heaven. There was no reason for me to live anymore. Then I started to pray. And God told me to go on living and do good things because that's what Martha would have wanted me to do.'

Jim paused, and then continued, 'So, I know how you feel, my friend. I know how much you loved Carla. I am telling you Frank, you have to go on living.'

I was still crying when I looked at Jim and said, 'How can I live, Jim? How can I? She died to save me. After these years, we finally found each other, now she is gone for good, and has left me alone. We were going to get married. We loved each other very much.'

'I know you did Frank, but you must get over it. It will take time. Carla is in heaven now, she's not coming back. You have to accept that.'

There was silence, and then Jim stood up and said, 'I did not tell you about my friend, the one I went to visit. He is the one that sent the FBI to help us. I didn't know the Chief of Police here in DC. I made that up. But my friend wants us to visit him any time you want. He's a very important man. I told him about you. We can go and visit him any time, and we can give him the video tape about Dr Kramer's research, and the tapes from Tom's office.

'You must trust him very much to give him these valuable tapes.'

'Yes Frank, I do trust him very much and he is a dear friend of mine; he is the President of the United States.'

Jim smiled and slowly walked out as I looked at him in astonishment.

Shortly after Jim left, I took a shower, sat down with a drink in one hand and Carla's photograph in the other hand. I was remembering her when I fell asleep.

CHAPTER TWENTY-ONE

As Jim left Frank's room, he stopped at the hotel bar for a drink before he went to bed. The hotel manager stopped him and told him, 'The hospital has called here multiple times and has asked for Frank, but he never answered the phone.'

'That's because he is very sad. His girlfriend died tonight.'

'Sorry to hear about that, but I thought it might be important. In fact it is important based on the caller's tone of voice. Here's the phone, could you call them?'

'Ok, I'll call them,' Jim said.

The hospital answered, and Jim said, 'My name is Jim. Someone from your hospital called for Frank tonight. He's the guy whose girlfriend died. He's very upset, and won't be able to talk now. Is there anything I can do?'

Jim was listening to the person answering the telephone, and then he said, 'You want me to come to the hospital now, urgently? (A pause.) OK, see you soon.'

He turned to the manager and said, 'The hospital told me they cannot talk over the phone, but they want me to come to the hospital right away. I am on my way to the hospital. Please don't disturb Frank.'

Jim drove to the hospital. A doctor escorted him to his office. He sat down and said, in an excited voice, 'Sometimes, in hospitals unusual things happen, possibly as a result of a mistake. I would like to tell you everything that happened since Frank's girlfriend, Carla, was brought in by the paramedics as a dead person, killed during the shootout. She was fully covered when she was brought to the autopsy room because she was dead awaiting autopsy. As the medic on duty entered the autopsy room, he bumped into a stranger wearing a doctor's coat who hurriedly exited the autopsy room. The medic didn't pay attention to the man at the time. However, shortly afterwards, as the medic was getting ready for the autopsy, he heard a noise that sounded like someone in pain. When he investigated, he found out that Carla was the one that was making the noise. He called the doctor and told him what had happened. The doctor and nurses took Carla from the autopsy room into a secluded room. Three doctors immediately came and checked her. It appears that when the paramedics took Carla from the scene, they did not check her condition properly. I guess the weather was bad and in their rush they assumed she was dead. But in reality, she did not die; she just passed out from the two bullet shots, one in the chest and one in her stomach. The three doctors are operating on her now to remove the two bullets. What I am trying to tell you is that the paramedics made a big mistake, but luckily the medic in the autopsy room heard a noise like someone in pain, doctors were called immediately, and she is being operated on as we speak. I hope Frank's not going to sue us, please tell him it was a mistake. This hospital cannot afford an expensive law suit.'

'This is what I am going to tell you now, doctor. If you don't do what I say, I will make sure Frank sues you. First, I don't want anybody to know she is alive, including Frank. Do you hear me? You can call her Jane Doe, but never reveal her name to anyone. And I do not want anybody to come near her room. Put a chair outside her door, then sit someone down on it, even yourself if you have to. Don't allow anybody to go in except for the doctors, do you understand? I plan to tell Frank when I know her true status, and it is the right time. Do you hear me?'

'Yes, clearly,' he answered.

'Remember, Carla is your responsibility, no more mistakes. Bring me a comfortable chair and put it by her bed. I plan to spend the night by her bed until she wakes up and I can hear her voice.'

An hour later the doctors came to see Jim. He asked them how Carla was, and one of them said, 'She's doing fine. She is coming out of surgery, and will need to rest for few days before she can go home. We cannot apologise enough for the mistake, and of course the hospital will make sure this type of mistake never happens again. And we will keep you informed. She is sedated, so it will be few hours before she wakes up and you can talk to her.'

'Thank you doctor. I'll stay by her bed until she wakes up. Also, please have someone bring me lots of coffee, and some water.'

#

In the morning, the team was waiting downstairs to go to the airport. I asked where Jim was. BJ answered, 'He probably took the red eye flight last night. He told me he had a lot to do back at his office.'

'That's unusual. I talked to him yesterday evening, and he didn't mention flying back early. I guess he saw me very sad last night and he didn't want to upset me. Oh well, we'll see him in San Diego.'

In the meantime, back in San Diego, I was having difficulty coping without Carla, especially now having to arrange for her funeral.

The day before the funeral, I was in the living room. I felt very tired, physically and mentally. So I stretched my legs out on the coffee table, rested my head on the back of the couch and closed my eyes. It must have been an hour later when I heard the doorbell ring. Oliver answered it. After a minute, Oliver came into the living room accompanied by a lady, richly dressed, with a beautiful little girl. Oliver introduced the lady as Mrs Donovan and her niece.

I stood up to greet them, 'Good morning, Mrs Donovan. Will you have a seat, please.'

Mrs Donovan and the little girl sat on the couch across from me.

'My name is Grace Donovan, I am Carla's older sister,' Mrs Donovan said. 'I live in San Francisco with my husband. We are here for the funeral. I am sorry my husband couldn't come.'

'You know, Mrs Donovan, just yesterday I was wondering whether Carla had any relatives. I am so glad you came. But why didn't you tell us you were coming? You could have stayed here with us.'

'That's OK, Frank, we came late last night and we went to a hotel. We were very tired. And by the way call me Grace.'

'Today, Grace, you and your niece are moving in here. This was Carla's house, so it is also yours. Oliver will move you here later on.'

'Thank you. Carla spoke so much about you, of course all in confidence.'

'Mrs Donovan, oh Grace, I only worshipped and loved one woman in my life. And that was Carla. I am so sad and lonely now that Carla has gone. I'm finding it difficult to live without her.'

'You shouldn't feel this way. I don't think Carla would have liked to see you unhappy.'

She paused for a minute. At the same time I turned my head towards the little girl; she was so beautiful, and she resembled Carla.

Grace saw me staring at the little girl. She turned and said, 'Frank, this is Jennifer, your daughter.'

I was stunned, lost for words. I slowly stood up and walked to Jennifer. The more I looked at her, the more I saw Carla.

Grace interrupted my concentration. 'This was the wedding surprise gift Carla was going to give you. Before she went to see you in Beverly Hills, Carla brought Jennifer to me and asked me to look after her. She was afraid something might happen to her. Carla was so happy that the three of you would be together. This is the moment she was waiting for since Jennifer was born; the moment of introducing Jennifer to you.

I was listening to Grace, but I kept staring at Jennifer. And as I approached her, I noticed that her eyes were blue, just like Carla's. But I also noticed they were wet and red; she must have been crying.

I slowly knelt in front of Jennifer, held her hands, and gently said, Hello Jennifer. Have you been crying?'

In a bashful and soft voice, Jennifer said, 'Yes, 'cause Mammy is not coming back.'

I was trying hard to control my emotions, when I said, 'Do you know I am your dad?'

'Yes, mammy told me. She also gave me this and told me not to lose it.' Jennifer handed me the heart-shaped pendant that I had given to Carla in Cairo. As I opened the pendant, Jennifer pointed to the pictures, and said, 'See, this is Mammy and this is you.'

That was too much for me to handle. I quickly hugged Jennifer, with tears pouring down my face. Jennifer hugged me too. Then slowly I moved Jennifer back and said, 'You are very beautiful and smart, just like your mother, and I loved your mother very much.'

'Mammy told me that she also loved you, very, very much,' Jennifer said.

I looked up to Grace; she had tears in her eyes. I then asked Jennifer, 'Would you like some milk and cookies?'

'Yes, please,' Jennifer replied in a soft voice.

I stood up, held her hand, and walked with her to the kitchen. I introduced her to Oliver, and told him to give Jennifer anything she wanted to eat and drink. I then returned to the living room.

I wiped my tears, sat next to Grace, and said, 'Grace, please tell me everything.'

Grace started to speak, 'About six weeks after returning from Cairo, Carla felt something was wrong. She visited the doctor, and after examination, he told her that she was pregnant. Before Carla left for Cairo, she didn't make love to her husband. I know that because Carla needed someone to talk to. We were very close, and she confided in me. Dr Kramer was always busy, travelling and working on his medical research. I suspect he knew Carla must have had an affair when he heard she was pregnant, but he did not make an issue of it; he blamed himself. He also knew that Carla was going to divorce him as soon as he finished his research. When Jennifer was born, Dr Kramer treated her as if she was his daughter.'

Grace wiped away her tears and continued, 'Carla didn't know where you were until she saw you on television during the kidnapping case. Soon after Dr Kramer was killed, Carla sat down with Jennifer and explained to her that Dr Kramer was not her real father. She told her that you were her father and gave her the pendant. Jennifer is smart, and she understood what Carla told her.'

'She's so beautiful, just like Carla. You know, I miss Carla so much,' I said.

'Frank, we all loved Carla, but she is not here. You are Jennifer's father, and you have to take care of her. You have to be strong. She needs you now more than ever. You know, Jennifer often wakes up in the middle of the night crying and calling for Carla.'

'Don't worry, Grace. I'll take good care of her.'

BJ, Rachel and Jackie came into the living room and I introduced them to Grace. At the same time, Oliver came in with Jennifer.

In a proud voice I told everybody, 'And this is Jennifer, Carla's daughter and my daughter.'

They all looked at me with surprise, while I added, 'Grace will explain everything, but right now I'm taking my daughter swimming. Come out when you finish.'

Back in DC, Jim was asleep on the chair waiting for Carla to come around. He woke up when he heard a voice calling him. He opened his eyes, and saw Carla wide awake but looking weak.

'Where am I,' she asked.

'You're in hospital being treated for gunshot wounds. Do you remember?'

'No, I thought I was dead in heaven.'

'You're in hospital. You had surgery to remove the bullets and you had some complications, but you are well now. All you need is rest.'

'Where's Frank and the rest of the team?'

'Carla, it's a long story, but you really died and through some miracle you came back and you are alive. The funny thing is that Frank is in San Diego with the team; they are arranging your funeral. They don't know you are alive. I am going to call him now and tell him to come over because I have a surprise for him - oh, and to cancel all the funeral arrangements.'

'Jim, call him now, I want to hear his voice.'

BJ was pouring a drink for everyone when the telephone rang. He answered it.

'Hi Jim, where are you, we left DC thinking you had already left for San Diego.'

There was a pause.

'You are where, still in DC? Wait, I'll call Frank.'

BJ called me over. When I took the phone from him, I heard Jim saying, 'Frank, now don't get excited, and I will explain later. Right now I want you to talk to someone, OK, it's real, are you relaxed, here is the phone.

I heard Carla's voice, 'Darling, where are you, I miss you so much.'

There was another pause, and then I shouted, 'Is that you Carla?'

'Yes darling, it's me. Could you come and take me home.'

'We're leaving right now.'

I hung up, looked at everybody, and shouted loudly, 'Carla is alive, she is not dead. We have to go to her now. BJ and Oliver, please charter a plane to take us all to DC today, right now. Don't worry about the cost, just get a plane now to take us to DC today, say around 4 or 5, and to take us back to San Diego, say tomorrow, anytime, whatever is OK with the pilot and the crew. Then I went to the pool area, and hugged Jennifer saying, 'I have good news for you. Are you ready? Your mother is not dead, she is alive in hospital. She is waiting for us. We are all going to DC today, and will bring her back with us.'

I went back to the living room and asked Jackie to please call everybody and cancel all the funeral arrangements, and if we had paid a deposit, to tell them to keep it, and not to forget to cancel the church also. Then

I walked to Grace and I said, 'Grace, you and Jennifer are coming with us. I'll have Oliver take you to your hotel and pack your luggage.'

'Frank, flying to DC now, that's a long journey.'

'Grace, you have to come with us. Your sister would love to see you. So, go now with Oliver, and when you come back, you can freshen up if you want, and then get ready for a wonderful journey. Don't forget to call your husband. I am sure Jackie and Rachel are pampering Jennifer.'

Grace smiled and thanked me.

BJ came up and said our flight was scheduled to leave around 5 o'clock. I was overwhelmed with joy.

Everybody gathered in the living room at 4 o'clock. Two limousines were waiting for us outside. Luggage was loaded, and we headed to the airport. Everybody was excited and smiling.

We arrived at the hangar where our plane was waiting. It was being refuelled and made ready for take-off. Luggage was loaded and we all boarded. It was about 5:10 when the pilot told us to buckle up.

The flight was smooth and comfortable. Jennifer sat next to me, and the team spread around. About two hours after we took off, the flight attendant announced that she would be serving a meal that consisted of chicken cordon blue with asparagus and roast potatoes, or filet mignon with mixed vegetables and roast potatoes. I asked Jennifer what she wanted to eat, and she said, 'I like chicken.'

'So, chicken for two,' I told the flight attendant.

After we finished eating, I asked the flight attendant if it was possible to speak to Jim at the hospital where Carla was being treated. A few minutes later, she came back, and handed me the phone saying, 'It's Jim.' I took the handset from her and said, 'Jim, is that you?'

'Yes, it's me. I just want to let you know Carla is doing very well, and is anxious to see you all.'

'We should arrive in DC in about two hours. You can check with the tower which area the plane will park, and have two limousines waiting to bring us to the hospital. After they drop us at the hospital, could you please tell the limousine drivers to take the luggage to the hotel. Thanks.'

'I'll do that. You can't imagine how happy Carla is. I will explain everything to you later. See you soon.'

'Jim, before you go, please don't tell Carla that her sister and daughter will be with us; it's a surprise. And one more thing. You remember that we have to visit the President, and we can't let him down. We must see him before we return to San Diego, so could you please arrange our visit to the White House, say for tomorrow or the day after tomorrow, whatever day the President wants. I have to thank him for sending those FBI agents to help us out. And you can brief him about what happened to Carla.'

'I understand what you're saying. Consider it done. I'll let you know when you arrive. And the limousines will be there. Bye for now.'

'Who was that on the phone?' BJ asked me.

'That was Jim, he's sitting next to Carla, and won't leave her side. He'll have two limousines waiting for us when we arrive. And he will arrange our meeting with the President. Once we do all that, we can return to San Diego.' Pointing at Jennifer I said, 'BJ, look at Jennifer, isn't she beautiful, just like her mother. I'm so happy, and I will take care of them.'

About two hours later, we heard the flight attendant announcing, 'It's time to buckle up, we will be landing in five minutes. And, by the way, you have all been a wonderful group. The pilot and I hope Carla gets well quickly, and you have a beautiful life together. Thank you, and we hope to see you again.'

'That was nice of her and the pilot,' Jennifer said.

'You are right darling, it was nice of them. Now, let's buckle up, we are about to land.'

The two limousines were waiting for us, and as soon as we came off the plane, I told the drivers to load the luggage, and take us to the hospital.

At the hospital, Grace, Jennifer and I rushed out of the limousine, and ran straight to the entrance where a nurse guided us to Carla's room.

We stood at the door, and slowly walked towards Carla. She was talking to Jim, and when she turned and saw us, we ran to her, and she hugged us, and gave me a kiss. It was like a kiss of life.

Hugging Jennifer, Carla said, 'So you finally met your father, I am so happy, isn't she beautiful?'

'Yes, she's like you, beautiful,' I agreed with Carla. Jennifer hugged her mother, and said, 'I missed you very much. Do you know when you can get out of this hospital?'

'Probably tomorrow. I've had so much rest, and I feel great. The doctors did a wonderful job in surgery.' Carla looked at Grace and said to her, 'Thank you for everything Grace. For taking Jennifer to see her father, and for bringing her here, and just being a wonderful loving sister. Come here, I want to hug you and kiss you.'

Grace went to Carla and they hugged and kissed each other.

A nurse came into the room to check on Carla. After she finished and left, I closed the door. Everybody else was still in the room. I looked at Carla, and I asked her, 'Carla, do you remember what happened that night at the RST Medical Center, when the shooting was going on, and Tom aimed at me, but you saw him, and ran towards me and threw yourself in front of the bullets. Do you remember that?'

'Yes, I remember all that.'

'Carla, do you remember what happened after that? Two bullets hit you in the chest and the stomach, and the ambulance took you to the hospital.'

'No, I don't remember anything after that. But it was very strange. I sensed that I was wearing a long white dress, surrounded by men and women also dressed in white. And suddenly I felt someone was rubbing my head, my stomach and my chest.'

'Do you remember who that was?' I asked Carla.

'Yes, while this person was massaging me, I opened my eyes, and I saw this young black man smiling at me. He had shining eyes that were mesmerising. He said a few words, something like, "You will feel better." Then he left.'

'You mean he massaged your head, stomach and chest, but never talked to you until just before he left and then you started to feel better?'

'That's about all,' Carla said.

'You all heard what she said. What do you make of it?' I asked everybody.

'I think she was saved by an angel,' Jennifer was the first to speak.

Everybody was quiet.

'Hello everybody,' I said, 'I think Jennifer gave us the best answer. So let's leave it at that and we won't talk about it anymore. It's definite: "CARLA WAS SAVED BY AN ANGEL".'

I asked Carla, 'When did the doctors say you could go home?'

'Tomorrow, but if I felt better, I could leave today,' Carla answered.

'Well, darling, how do you feel now?'

'I feel great.'

'Then we should call the doctor and tell him that.'

Jim called for the doctor and asked him if Carla could go home today. The doctor said, 'Yes, she can go. We have never seen a person recover so fast from two gunshot bullets. It's a miracle. We wish her all the best.' Then the doctor left.

'Well, you heard the doctor. Let's take her to the hotel.'

At the hotel, and before everybody went to their rooms, I suggested we meet at the hotel restaurant in half hour. Everybody agreed.

Grace said that she would call her husband and tell him the funeral had been cancelled, and that she would explain everything when she saw him.

We all met at the hotel restaurant for dinner. It was such a wonderful dinner celebrating Carla and showing our love for her. Carla ate just a little.

At the end of the dinner, Jim told me that the President would meet us the following day at 1 o'clock in the afternoon in the White House. I was happy about that.

'Jim, I assume we will all be there, including Carla, Jennifer, Grace, and also Charlie and Madoda.'

'Yes, of course, Frank, everybody. I'll have the limousine pick Charlie and Madoda and bring them to the White House. And please don't forget the video tapes of the complete research, and the tapes from Tom's office. He needs them so the government can prosecute Tom, Steve, Ramsey and Scott.'

'Well, since everything is organised, we might as well arrange for the flight back to San Diego late tomorrow, say around 5 o'clock.'

'Don't worry, Frank, BJ and I will take care of everything. You just take care of Carla.'

Carla and Jennifer approached us as we were talking. Jennifer came to me and I lifted her up in my arms and said, 'How would you like to meet the President of the United States tomorrow?'

'Ooh, that would be great. Can I have a picture with him, and get his autograph?'

'Oh my, you are such a clever girl. Yes, we will have a picture with him and he will sign it.'

'But now, Jennifer, it's time for bed, for tomorrow you will be very busy,' Carla said as we bid Jim goodnight.

Carla and I put Jennifer in bed and covered her up. We left her room and I just couldn't wait to put my arms around Carla and give her a passionate kiss.

'Darling,' Carla said, 'we can't make love tonight. I still have some pain in my stomach and chest, and I don't want to mess up the stitches.'

'Well, we can undress, you sit on my lap, and we kiss. I just miss you around me and miss your lips and naked body.'

'I love that, I missed you Frank, so much.'

And we went on kissing.

#

We all met at the restaurant in the morning and had breakfast.

Everybody seemed hungry. After breakfast, I suggested we pack our bags and check out of the hotel because after we met the President we would go directly to the airport and fly home.

The limousine drove us through the White House gates, and we were escorted by the Secret Service to the Oval Office. It wasn't long before the President came in, smiling and jolly. He walked directly to Jim and shook his hand saying, 'How are you buddy? I don't see you for years, and now I see you three times in a few days. Come, introduce me to your friends.'

Jim introduced me to the President. The President shook my hand, paused while looking at me, and said, 'Jim told me everything. I want to thank you and your team for what you did. I know you are British, that's great, we are all brothers. But seriously, you have all given tremendous service to this country, and to all those people dying of this vicious decease. Maybe we finally have a solid reliable cure, thanks to you and especially Dr Kramer and his two associates. Having said that, I don't want to forget Carla, a courageous woman. She played an important role; without her we would have never uncovered this conspiracy. Now look at that guy,' he pointed to Jim, 'if it wasn't for him, I wouldn't be here today. He risked his life to save me and other soldiers when we were on active service in the Army together, something I will never forget. I will do anything for him, and we will always be the best of friends, like best brothers. On top of that, he is modest and kind, and he will not agree to come and work for me. He said he likes San Diego. I don't blame him; they have excellent weather there.'

Then the President looked at me and added, 'Did you know he was decorated with the Congressional Medal of Honour?'

'No, I did not know that, Mr President,' I said giving him a surprise look. 'Jim is a great but modest man, and he doesn't like to be glorified.'

Jim then introduced Carla, her daughter Jennifer and her sister Grace to the President.

'Well, Carla, you are a very courageous woman, risking your life to save your future husband. I admire that. Without you and your determination, we wouldn't have uncovered this situation. And this is Jennifer, a beautiful smart girl.' The President bent down to shake her hand, saying, 'You must be proud of your mother. Oh I forgot, I am to take a picture with you, see the photographer is already here, and as soon as he develops it, I'll autograph it for you. You know, one day you could become the President of the United States. Remember, nothing is impossible.'

The President turned to Grace and said, 'I want to thank you for helping Carla through these hard times. You must be proud of her.'

'Yes, Mr President. She is a wonderful sister and my best friend.'

Jim then went to introduce the rest of the team to the President. 'Mr President, this is the team that risked their life to put these bad guys in jail.'

'What can I say, BJ, Oliver, Jackie and Rachel, you were all super and anybody would be proud to have you as a friend. I am your friend, and I want to meet you again. I can't thank you enough.'

It appeared to me that the President was a gentle man, a friendly type who cared for the welfare of people, and one who I felt we could trust with the tapes.

Jim then introduced Charlie to the President, 'I am so glad to meet you Charlie. Jim told me all about you.'

'I hope it's all good,' Charlie said.

'Oh yes, very, very good, and I like you Charlie. I want to thank you for all your dedicated help. Any friend of Jim is my friend. If you ever want to join my staff, you just come and see me, the job is yours. Remember that, I mean it.'

'Thank you Mr President, Charlie said, 'I might take you up on that.'

The last person Jim introduced to the President was Madoda. The President shook Madoda's hand, and kept holding it, saying, 'You know Madoda, I admire you. You've gone through hell with those four men, and suffered a lot. But you stuck with your belief. You knew they were bad and greedy, and killers, but you kept with what you believed in. Fate brought this to an end, thanks to Frank, Carla, and the team. They like you, and their utmost desire was to get these men to face justice for what they did, and for you to be rescued before they killed you. I believe in fate Madoda, and I believe in you. You are an honest man, and have been a tremendous help to this country. I will notify my immigration authorities to help you get citizenship as soon as possible, and I would be proud to sign my agreement. If you need any assistance with anything, just call Jim or call me, OK? I wish you all the best. I know you will make an honest good citizen.'

While the President was talking to Madoda, Carla happened to look at their direction, and she opened her eyes wide, and pulled on my shirt, saying, 'Frank, look.'

I turned to her and asked, 'Look at what?'

Carla said, 'You see that man talking with the President? He's the man who was rubbing my head, my stomach, and my chest, when I was in the autopsy room. I felt the pain going away after he left.'

'Are you sure?' I asked.

'Yes, I'm one hundred percent sure of that. He was the person who was touching me.'

'That's Madoda, the man we rescued from the RST Medical Center. Wait here, I have to see Jim.'

I went to talk to Jim. 'Jim, something very unusual happened. Carla just told me that the man talking to the President just now, Madoda, is actually the same man who was massaging her head, stomach and chest in the autopsy room. She said the pain started to go away right after he left her. I believe he must have some sort of spiritual magic or something. Before we go to the airport, could we talk to him, can you arrange it?'

'Yes, I can. Let's wait until we leave the White House because whatever power Madoda has, maybe he doesn't want it advertised. We need to respect that. So we'll see him later.'

I noticed the President was waving at me, so I walked towards him. He pulled me to one side and said, 'Frank, I can't thank you enough. I like you and your team, and I want to be your friend.' Then he came closer to me and whispered, 'If I ever needed help without any fuss or publicity, could I get in touch with you?'

Yes, Mr President. Anytime you need us, just let Jim know,' I replied.

'Thank you Frank, I wanted to hear you say that. And if at any time, you want to talk to me, or need anything without interference by anyone in the White House, just call the White House operator and tell the person who answers the telephone that you want to speak to "Yogi Bear". They will know what to do. It's a code for special people trying to contact me.'

I smiled and said, 'Thank you Yogi Bear, I'll remember that.'

Just before we left, the President wanted to take a picture with all of us. So, we gathered around the President and the photographer took the pictures.

'I'll send you copies when they're ready,' he promised.

We said goodbye to the President and left for the special lounge at the airport to await our departure.

Jim called everybody to join him in a corner of the lounge. As soon as we got together, I spoke to Madoda, in front of everybody. 'Carla was pronounced dead, and she was in the autopsy room. She told me she opened her eyes, and saw you rubbing her head, her stomach and her chest. And before long, the pain started to go away. If you don't want to explain we'll understand, but all of us want to thank you for what you did bringing Carla back to life.'

Carla stood by Madoda and said, 'I especially want to thank you, because you didn't only save me, but you saved Frank, my future husband, Jennifer, my daughter, and Grace, my sister. You made our lives happy again. You gave us life. You don't have to explain, and I promise you that nobody will ever know about what happened in the autopsy room.'

Madoda looked at us with his shining eyes and said, 'My father had a strange power. He didn't know how he got it, but he used it few times to save people. He told me that I might have the same power because it might be hereditary. When I was kidnapped, tortured, and beaten, I thought of that power, but I was weak, and I couldn't think. When I saw what happened at the centre, and then you being shot and dead, I couldn't accept that, and I was aware of some strange things happening to me. So when I found out where you were taken, to the autopsy room, I had to go there and try to see if I could do something. I started massaging your head, then your stomach, then your chest. I kept doing that over and over, praying at the same time and thinking of my father. Then I heard someone coming so I rushed out, bumping into the person coming in. I went to the men's room and I washed my face; I was sweating. When I felt better, I walked outside, and I saw all these nurses and doctors running to your room. At that moment I knew you were healed, and I was so happy.'

Listening to him, Carla was in tears, she then looked at him and said, 'You are a brave man, and I respect and adore your courage. I want you to remember, you saved my life, and from now on, you are my brother. I wish you could come with us. Remember, my house is your house, come anytime, do you understand?' Carla asked him.

'Yes, I do,' answered Madoda. 'I'm going to be busy getting my American citizenship. Once that is done, I will definitely come and see you. Maybe I can join your team.'

'That would be wonderful. You can join our team anytime you want,' I said. 'Come and see us very soon, and don't forget. By the way, as soon as you get your phone, call us with the number. We love you Madoda.'

'I love you all, you are my family,' Madoda said.

Carla walked to Madoda; she hugged him and kissed him on the cheeks.

We said goodbye to Charlie and Madoda, then we boarded our flight. We waved goodbye to them, and they kept waving.

CHAPTER TWENTY-TWO

We entered the house, everybody was quiet.

I noticed the mood, so I said, 'Ok you guys, I know we are here, but our hearts are still in Washington DC.

As I spoke I heard Carla sobbing, and Grace, Jennifer and myself went to comfort her.

'Sorry, but I'm very emotional at the moment. I was thinking of Madoda; he's such a nice guy, and what he did for me, and for all of you, he gave us life and something to look forward to. I really admire him.'

'I agree with you Carla,' I commented. 'He's now officially a member of this team. I am sure Jackie and Rachel, BJ and Oliver all agree.'

In a loud voice, Jennifer said, 'I agree too.'

'To change the subject, when Madoda gets his citizenship and comes here, we should all fly to Wales, and visit my wonderful town of Rhyl. Carla and Jennifer would love to see where I was born, and where BJ and I met, and all the beautiful sights in and around Rhyl. Would you and your husband like to join us, Grace, when we go to Wales?'

'I think that would be a great holiday for us. We've heard so much about Wales, so count us in.'

'Great, and we'll invite Jim and Charlie. I'm sure they'll like that. We'll hire a private jet to take us to Wales, and bring us back two weeks later. I have a large house with plenty of rooms that are not being used. You'll also meet Jane and Joseph, the caretakers of my house. They are family to me. You'll love them and love their food. Maybe Oliver will get some new recipes from Jane. Anyway, what do you think?'

They all shouted. 'AGREED,' and I heard BJ say, 'Hurry home, Madoda!'

Everybody went to their rooms, and Carla and I put Jennifer in bed. When the place was quiet, I poured two glasses of Chivas Regal, and Carla and I sat on the couch.

'Carla, my darling, we have a lot of time to make up. I missed you so much. And Jennifer, my baby, we'll take good care of her. Now I have two babies and I love them both.' We hugged and kissed, I couldn't resist those beautiful lips.

Carla said, 'I think it's time for us to go to bed, and have some love time. But you have to be a bit careful.'

'Of course I'll be careful, let's not waste time.'

Holding onto each other, we slowly walked upstairs. I felt on top of the world; I had my Blue Eyes, and I had Jennifer.

Madoda's
MAGIC

9 781805 411727